Tempting the Dhampir

ELLE STERLING

MONSTERS OF ALBERAD

Tempting the Dhampir

Dedication

TO ALL THOSE WHO AREN'T AFRAID
TO HYPE OTHERS UP. FOR MAKING
SPACE AND CELEBRATING
EACH OTHER.

Content Warning

THIS BOOK IS LIGHT AND SMUTTY, AND IS INTENDED FOR ADULT READERS 18+.

SHOULD YOU HAVE ANY SPECIFIC QUESTIONS ABOUT TRIGGERS, PLEASE DON'T HESITATE TO REACH OUT TO ME AT ELLE@ELLESTERLING.COM FOR MORE DETAILS.

IF ANY OF THE FOLLOWING ELEMENTS MAKE YOU UNCOMFORTABLE, PLEASE PROCEED WITH CAUTION:

STRONG LANGUAGE
EXPLICIT SEX
BITING
SPANKING
MENTION OF DECEASED FAMILY MEMBER
(BRIEF AND OFF PAGE)
EMOTIONALLY ABUSIVE RELATIONSHIP
(NOT BETWEEN MAIN CHARACTERS)

Sadie

I'm so happy to have an excuse to get all dolled up tonight," I say excitedly to my sister as I wind a section of my long blonde hair around the curling iron.

The music blasting from my phone echoes my mood as I dance in my seat in front of my travel mirror propped on the table.

Cece stares out at the slice of sea visible from our balcony window but turns at my words. "I've got a good feeling about tonight," she sighs dreamily, reflecting my sentiments.

"Oh yeah. Sunset. Cruise. Island. Party." I punch each word out, my anticipation bubbling over into every syllable.

Cece glides toward the faded blue armchair next to me and gracefully lowers herself into the seat. She brings her long blonde hair forward over one shoulder and starts running her fingers through her natural waves.

"It still feels unreal being on vacation in the Caribbean, never mind being lucky enough to get invited along on a ladies' night out on the water," she says with a slight shake of her head, a gentle smile curving her rosy lips.

I reach forward and lower the volume so I can hear Cece's dulcet tones better.

Nodding, I say, "Meeting Iris and Helena at the beach bar earlier this week was really cool. Them inviting us on their chartered cruise is mind-blowingly awesome." Amazement coats my words as I target my curtain bangs next, wrapping some strands around my iron.

Iris and Helena were seated at the table next to ours at lunch, and we soon got to chatting, which led to joining tables and sharing life stories. We ended up hanging out together until closing time and exchanging contact details.

Cece's hands pause midway in her hair. Her eyebrows draw together as she emphatically says, "Right? They're so generous. I'm sorry for Helena's heartbreak, but Iris organizing a breakup celebration is a new level of friendship right there."

I finish the final section of my hair and carefully put the hot curling iron down.

Pivoting in my wooden chair to continue the conversation face-to-face, I arch an eyebrow at Cece. "I'd totally organize a special event for you too. But maybe not at their level of luxury, though." I can't quite meet Cece's eyes as I admit, "A teacher's salary can only stretch so far."

I chuckle to hide my grimace, thinking about how long it would take me to save up for the type of yacht Iris chartered for tonight.

Sitting up straighter, Cece lays a comforting hand on my forearm and gently says, "I'd never expect you to. Besides, if it came to it, you know I'd much rather have a picnic out in nature with wine and cheese."

I cover Cece's hand with mine, the corners of my mouth turning up with appreciation for my big sis. "Too true. I'd organize the best picnic. All the wine, all the cheese."

Cece's laugh tinkles through the air. "I know you would. And I'd organize a big glitter fest for you, with loud music and lots of dancing."

My giggles join hers, and I singsong, "Which is basically

what tonight is."

I close my eyes and squeal through pressed lips, my foot bouncing against the floor in excitement.

Cece's eyes are bright as she sits back and crosses one leg over the other. "I'm looking forward to meeting the other women they invited. I wonder where everyone is from."

"Me too. They said there'll be about ten of us, right?" I ask, tilting my head as I think back to the conversations and how the night came to be.

Iris, Helena's ride-or-die bestie, arranged a post-breakup trip for her to the Caribbean and, as the cherry on top, organized tonight as the main event. They invited some women they met throughout the week to join them and make it a proper celebration before heading back to Florida.

Cece nods, her eyes widening as she blows out a slow breath. "Yeah, ten total. That's a lot of energy in one place."

I reach out and squeeze her hand. "Don't worry, I'm sure you'll find a moment to recharge your social batteries. Maybe a couple of minutes of quietly staring at the sunset once we get to the beach will help."

With soft eyes and a voice rich with gratitude, Cece says, "It definitely would. Thanks for understanding me so well. This is *so* your scene, you're probably already planning your moves for a dance-off."

My grin is wide as I answer, "My stomach has been a fluttery mess all day. There's just something about tonight that has me feeling tingly all over. Now, let's pick outfits."

I grab Cece's hand and lead her to the small closet stuffed with our vacation outfits. My short, bright dresses hang next to her long, muted ones, a clear distinction of our personalities. I move my hand along her flowy maxi dresses before settling on her favorite color and pulling out the lilac dress.

"This one," I say confidently and hold it out to her.

"I don't think this one screams fancy boat party. Do you

think it'll work?" Cece asks quietly, hand tentatively reaching out toward the beautiful dress with its small embroidered flowers along the bust.

I duck my head to meet her gaze and offer her a small smile. "I say, wear whatever makes you happy. There's no one to impress tonight. No boys allowed, remember? Besides, you look absolutely stunning in that dress."

Cece's ivory skin pinkens as a delighted smile stretches across her face. "If you say so." With a definitive nod, she takes the dress from me and holds it against her body, one hand gliding across the floral chiffon fabric. "This really is my favorite dress. I love how I feel in it." Looking up at me, she says, "You've always been good at knowing what will look good on people and what suits their personalities."

"Thanks, Cece."

Her words hit me straight in the chest, warmth crawling up my neck and staining my cheeks.

I love pretty dresses and making women feel good about themselves. Styling my sister and friends for parties comes naturally to me. But it's never been a career I could afford to pursue.

"What are you going to wear?"

Cece's question yanks me back into the present, and with a subtle shake of my head to clear any lingering thoughts about my dream job, I take out my pink minidress. "What do you think about this one?"

My sister's lips tilt into a rare smirk. "I think all those extra squats before this trip are definitely worth showing off in that number."

I straighten my back and do a little shimmy. A warm, contented feeling spreads through me with the knowledge that the hard work I've put in is paying off, and I reply, "I hated doing them at first, but I love how they make me feel."

"Well, you look fantastic with your peachy butt," Cece says cheerfully.

"And you look beautiful with your willowy elegance," I admit.

I have always loved how Cece and I embrace our differences and support each other. She's so graceful and kind, and she motivates me to be a good sister and friend. Something that doesn't come easily to my more critical, outspoken nature. For all Cece's sweetness, I more than make up for it with my spice, and I've landed myself in quite a few tricky spots over the years because of my runaway mouth.

Refocusing on tonight, I say, "Let's talk accessories." I squint my eyes and tilt my head as I envision the ensemble and what would look best. "You need a bikini under that dress in case we have to wade through water to get from the island to the beach."

"Yes! That's smart thinking." Cece goes to the curtains and draws them closed before putting on her crochet bikini.

The afternoon light is bright enough to filter through the beige curtains, but I turn on a small light anyway before slipping into my skintight mini.

"Are you going to wear your fancy pink stilettos?" Cece asks me, knowing how much I love my fuchsia *Jimmy Choo Averly 100* pumps with their delicate ankle straps and oversized organza bows. I had saved up for months to get those beauties for myself and only wear them on special occasions.

"I wish, but no. Taking them on the beach is just asking to ruin them and I refuse to commit shoe murder." My dainty heels deserve plush carpeting or hardwood floors to show off their beauty, not sand on those pretty bows and—god forbid—scuff marks on their soles. "Besides, shoes usually aren't allowed on boats. I saw it on a reality show I watched."

Cece finishes putting on her clothes and turns to me. "What do you think?"

I give her an appreciative once-over. "Your tits look spectacular, and your legs look like they go on for days. With your hair down just like that, you're all kinds of elven princess aesthetic goals.”

She seems genuinely pleased with my assessment, if her wide smile is anything to go by. “You’re the best little sister ever. I’m keeping you.” Gesturing with a finger up and down my body, she adds, “You look absolutely ravishing in that. The sparkles on the shoulder straps add that extra oomph you like.”

This time it’s my turn to beam at her. “With compliments like that, I’ll be keeping you around too.”

Chuckling, Cece moves to the full-length mirror and starts humming a vaguely familiar melody while finger combing her beachy waves. With her hair long enough to reach the small of her back and its naturally sun-kissed shade of pale blonde, she really does look ethereal.

I pad over to the curtains and open them again, needing the natural light to finish my makeup, and move to the table holding my beauty supplies. Bending forward to position my face closer to the travel mirror, I try to apply the smoothest flick to my eyeliner that I can muster, despite the slight quivers of anticipation moving through my hand.

“Do you want to borrow any makeup?” I call to Cece as I finish up.

I think I might inadvertently have shares in Sephora at this stage in my quest to achieve the ultimate no-makeup makeup look. Special nights out are for a bold lip or a strong cat eye to make my blue eyes pop, the extra effort adding some pep to my step.

“Can I maybe borrow some lip gloss? I’m still deciding if I want to go through the effort of putting on mascara,” Cece asks, not one to habitually wear anything but sunscreen on her face.

I grab a pink nude shade with a pearly gloss and join her in front of the mirror. Staring at our reflection, I can’t help but think we make such a cute pair, with my bright pink complementing her pastel lilac.

Our heads instinctively lean toward each other, and we share a grin.

"You ready for the best night ever?" I ask, my heart pounding so hard with excitement that it feels like my insides are vibrating.

Cece's eyes gleam as she gives me a toothy smile. "Oh yeah. Let me grab my shoes, it's about time we leave."

With a final peek in the mirror, I check my teeth, fluff my curtain bangs, and give my raspberry-pink lips a quick smack before I slip on some appropriate footwear and follow my punctual sister out of our hotel room.

Tonight is going to be memorable. I can feel it in my soul.

Sadie

Cece and I make our way down to the dock, our shoes clopping along the wooden slats jutting out over the water. "Isn't this magnificent?" Cece whispers, her steps slowing to a stop.

I take in the view and my jaw goes slack. We're both momentarily rendered speechless as we gaze out at the Caribbean Sea.

The wind is barely stirring today, making the water appear almost lazy with its tranquil waves lapping gently against the shore. The cerulean-blue water is beckoning us to board our boat and venture farther out, to where the sunset is sure to paint the most picturesque scene of pinks and oranges dancing on its sparkly surface. Around the bay, palm trees bend toward the sea, leaning down, straining, as if they want to answer the ocean's call.

Tonight I feel like one of those palm trees. There's something stirring in my gut, calling me, drawing me to the horizon, promising something magical.

"Look, that must be them," I say to Cece once I wrench my eyes away from the view.

I point at a group of women standing on the dock, excitedly chatting with each other, right in front of a fancy-looking boat. The varying styles and colors of their outfits are a feast to my eyes, and I grab Cece's arm to speed us toward them.

With each step closer to our hosts, my pulse races faster, my hips already swaying to the beat coming from the boat.

Iris is the first to notice us. "Florence, Sadie, we're so happy you could make it." She takes turns to wrap us in hugs. "You two are looking gorgeous, don't you think, Lenny?"

Helena steps away from the conversation she was in and is quick to hug us too. "Thank you for coming," she says with a relaxed smile as she steps back. "You both look beautiful."

Helena's eyes are gleaming with a brightness that was absent the last time I saw her. This trip seems to be the healing experience she needed.

I squeeze her hand. "No way we would've missed it. I've been looking forward to tonight since you told us about it. And by the way, violet is definitely your color."

Shifting my gaze to Iris, I flick my finger up and down, indicating her outfit, and nod my approval. "Lady, that emerald green is magic on you."

Iris spreads her arms and does a little twirl. "We chose our outfits based on the mini color analysis you did for us at the bar. Sadie, you've missed your calling. Maybe you should consider a career change." She lets the words hang and quirks an eyebrow.

I swallow around a sudden lump in my throat. She has no idea how close that hits.

I force my lips into a smile and bring the focus back to our hosts. "How did you meet all the women you've invited? Same as us—right place, right time?" I ask, gesturing to the women lucky enough to be included in such a once-in-a-lifetime opportunity.

Iris nods and explains, "Once we got the contact for the chartering company, we looked at the yachts they had to offer. I wanted to go big for one last celebration. However, it felt weird to have such an extravagant yacht for just the two of us. We decided that if we met anyone throughout the week—particularly women, because right now we need some distance from men—and if we clicked with them, we would invite them along."

With a practiced ease of friends used to finishing each other's sentences, Helena continues, "You would think it would be hard, but it all happened very organically. We met them at a restaurant"—she gestures to two women—"and lay next to those three on the beach." She waves at a group of three girls around my age. "And Cordelia we met at our hotel," she tacks on while pointing to a leggy blonde.

Iris picks up Helena's thread again. "Everyone is super keen for a ladies' night and helping me get my bestie into a new, to-be-defined era. She's officially done with her loser-boyfriend era." She raises her volume on the final sentence, and a bunch of whoops follow from the girls.

Cece lays a hand on Iris's arm. "We are so grateful to be included."

With a warm smile, Iris says, "Honestly, it feels like the universe was working in our favor. Nothing has ever gone so smoothly with my planning."

"No, no, no." Helena jumps forward and playfully places a hand over Iris's mouth. "We don't say things like that. It's like you're inviting trouble. Just quietly thank the universe, or fate, or whatever you want, but we're not here to lay down any kinds of challenges."

All the women within earshot start laughing, but some laughs sound a bit strained.

I won't let any negativity enter my mind tonight. This good feeling I've had all day is still bubbling in my chest, and I'm going to focus on that.

"Here, come meet some of the women." Iris leads Cece and me to two of the women she pointed to earlier. "Natalie, Diana, this is Sadie and Florence. You ladies chat while I go check on the boat."

"This is the coolest shit that has ever happened to me. How about you guys? Get invited onto yachts on the regular?" Natalie asks, cherry-red lips curled into a smile.

She's got a very goth-chic aesthetic that looks amazing on her, tattoos peeking out from under the hem of her pleated skirt and the left sleeve of her white T-shirt.

"It's definitely a first for us too." Cece laughs. "Where are you from?"

Natalie scrunches her nose. "Arizona-ish. I'm currently backpacking and don't have a final destination in mind. Guess I'll see where life takes me after this." She shrugs like it's no big deal.

Diana tilts her head to the side, her eyebrows drawing together for a second before shooting up into an arch. She nods as she says, "That's really inspirational. I'm currently on this new journey of just saying fuck it and going along with whatever life wants to throw at me. I mean, I still can't quite believe they just invited a bunch of random people and paid for us all. Feels like there's a catch somewhere. Yet, here I am." She raises her arms out wide.

"You know what, Diana? I might just join you on that journey. From now on, I'll say fuck it and see where life takes me. As long as there are no cults. That's a hard line for me." I quickly add the last part before I'm swept up in some weird shit.

"That makes three of us. Let's cheers our imaginary drinks until we get the proper stuff on the yacht. You in, Florence?" Natalie sticks her hand forward, cupping an imaginary glass.

Cece hesitates for a second, then says, "Sure, why not. It's about time I step out of my comfort zone." She raises her hand to join the toast.

The four of us clink our fictional champagne flutes, anticipation for tonight amping up to a new level.

Iris appears on the ramp and raises her voice for all of us to hear. "Okay, ladies. All aboard! Leave your shoes in the box before getting on, grab a flute of champagne, and find a spot to enjoy the cruise. Our captain will drop us off at a beach on a secluded island in about an hour, and then we'll make cocktails and have finger foods once we get on shore."

Another chorus of whoops meets her statement as we board the boat.

After checking that Cece is comfortable, I move to the bow to meet some of the other women.

"Love your dress!" a woman in a yellow off-the-shoulder romper calls to me, giving me a thumbs-up.

I amble toward her and indicate with my champagne flute. "I love yours. Yellow is a great choice for your complexion," I compliment right back. "I'm Sadie."

Her smile is broad and welcoming. "I'm Alice. This is Louisa and Sylvia." She motions to her two friends. "Please, sit."

I plop down next to them and ask, "How do you girls know each other?"

"We were college roommates, and this is a reunion trip of sorts," Louisa explains.

She has an athletic build and is wearing super cute cut-off jeans, making her toned legs look even longer.

Sylvia, dressed in a silky red slip dress, elaborates, "We all chose different careers and had to move away from each other, but we stay in touch."

"Ah, that sucks that you couldn't stay together. What kind of careers do you have?" I ask, angling my head so my hair streams out behind me in the wind.

A gentle smile crinkles Sylvia's eyes, pride lacing her voice as she points to each of her friends. "Alice works in STEM and Louisa is a physical therapist. I'm an art history major, currently unemployed. How about you?"

My eyebrows shoot up at their diverse and impressive professions. "Three very smart ladies. I'm a teacher," I state.

"Four very smart ladies, thank you very much," Alice chimes in.

"I'll drink to that." I thrust my glass forward, and the women clink theirs to it.

I spend the rest of the ride hopping from conversation to conversation, getting to know all the women. All too soon, we make it to the most breathtaking island.

A beach of the purest white sand greets us. The water is a brilliantly clear aquamarine, fading into a light celeste blue as we approach the beach. Palms and lush vegetation decorate the shore, calling us to explore the island.

"You said this island is uninhabited?" I think it's Diana who asks once we drop anchor.

"That's what we've been told," Iris says with a reassuring smile.

One by one, the women step down from the back of the boat, into the shallows. A hum of pleasure escapes me as I lower myself down into the lukewarm water reaching me high on my thighs. Holding my drink up, I wiggle my toes into the soft sand, the water clear enough to see my sparkly pink toes peeking through.

"Cece, hand me your drink. You're going to want to hike that dress up," I call to my sister, the gentle waves lapping at my bare legs.

"Thanks, Dede," she says, giving me her flute before pulling the skirt of her dress up and lowering herself down next to me.

All the women band together to get the supplies to the shore, taking turns to wade through the tranquil shallows while balancing snacks and drinks above the waterline.

"I've got the ice," Natalie shouts.

I smile at that. I've noticed her frequently running ice cubes down her arms. Wonder if she's got an ice kink.

A few trips back and forth, and we've got the blankets, cushions, and picnic tables set up. Helena arranges the food, and Iris the drinks.

By the time we finish setting up, the sun has lowered in the sky, already streaking the blue with hues of pink and gold. The colors reflect beautifully off the surface of the water, making it look as if the sun is dancing atop the sea.

I walk over to Cece, who's standing right where the ocean meets the beach, listless waves licking at her feet as she stares at the most beautiful sky I've ever seen.

Cece takes a deep breath and lets it out on a slow exhale. "Isn't it the most enchanting sight?" she asks, a wistful expression playing across her face.

She's undoubtedly trying to memorize the colors for her next big embroidery piece.

"You want to thread paint it, don't you?" I ask, burying my toes into the sand next to hers.

Cece's gaze stays fixed on the horizon, her brow furrowed as she says, "Absolutely. I want to take a picture, but also not. It won't do it justice. I keep thinking about which threads I'd have to layer to even remotely come close to capturing this. But it's captivating me."

I slip my hand into Cece's and turn to face her. "You're such a talented artist, I'm sure you'll figure it out. Just like you did with that piece of the woman dancing in the forest. It's imprinted in my brain. Your best work yet." I rub at my chest with my free hand, emotion bubbling just underneath the surface. "I'm so proud of you. When I showed your website to Iris and Helena, I could literally feel my chest puffing up more with each piece they saw."

Cece's whole face lights up, and she stands a little straighter. Tucking a piece of her waist-length hair behind her ear, she gives me a delighted smile. "That's my favorite embroidery piece I've ever done. The whole scene came to me in a vivid dream. I don't know if you noticed, but the woman dancing in the meadow looks similar to me." Cece rolls her lips between her teeth as pink stains her cheeks. "I *know* the scene can't be real, but it *felt* real. Like it was in a past or future life. It was like I could feel the crisp fall air on my skin, even now as I recall the dream. I could smell the fresh forest air, the grass, the trees. Oh, the trees." Her eyes take on a dreamy glaze as she recalls every detail. "There were shades of mustard, amber, rust, ginger, olive, brick red even..."

"Do you still have it?"

"I haven't had the heart to sell it yet," Cece admits. Her lips turn down at the corners, and a hint of sadness tinges her voice.

"Well, maybe you're meant to keep it," I say decisively. "I love what a great artist you are and how you've developed your craft, how you can paint with thread and bring a picture to life on fabric. I'm also proud of you for being a savvy small business owner, for turning your art into a living."

Cece surges forward to hug me, but in her usual gentle way—knowing not to mess with the hair I spent an hour curling. I return her hug with just as much fervor.

After a moment, Cece steps back and cups my shoulders. "Sisters by blood."

I cup her shoulders back. "Friends by choice," I finish our mantra, beaming.

Letting go of Cece, I close my eyes and cringe at what I'm about to ask. "Soooo, not to ruin this beautiful moment, but you don't suppose an uninhabited island has facilities, do you? The champagne seems to have gone right through me. Do you maybe want to come with me, just through those trees?" I squint one of my eyes open, my shoulders still high around my ears, knowing it's a big ask to walk away from this view.

"Dede," Cece says on a sigh.

"We'll be quick." I give her the best puppy dog eyes I can muster.

"Let's go." She gives me an indulgent smile. "I'd like to be back in time to catch the last remnants of the rays dancing on the surface, though. I have an idea to highlight the water with this very thin gold thread..." And Cece's off in her own world, already designing her next pièce de résistance.

On our way toward the lush vegetation, I let Natalie know where we're going.

"Watch out for any lurking predators!" she shouts with a laugh.

It's highly unlikely that there's anything dangerous on the island, but one can never be too careful. All of us probably have at least one story of carrying car keys between our fingers, or waiting for a message from a friend to see if they made it home safe after a night out.

After a couple of paces through the underbrush, Cece stops to look at some peculiar flowers. She lowers onto her haunches and gestures at the blue flowers with their teensy bioluminescent glow, trailing deeper into the forest. I remain standing right behind her, wary of the flowers that look like they're from a sci-fi movie.

"Aren't they beautiful?" Cece's voice is thick with wonder as she inspects them without touching. "It looks like they're growing in some kind of path. I've never seen anything like it."

"Should we call the others to come look?" I ask.

I'm no botanist, but even I can appreciate their uniqueness. Maybe the other women would too.

"Let's venture a tad farther in, and then we can get the others. I have a feeling there's something even more special waiting up ahead for us." Cece rarely does anything remotely selfish, so I really want to indulge her in this flower quest.

"No need to try and convince me. You know I'm always up for an adventure." My smile builds until it's a full grin and those flutters in my stomach return tenfold.

Cece shares my grin, sunset view all but forgotten. "Let's just step carefully, we don't want any kinds of thorns stabbing into our bare feet."

"Good idea. Tippy toes, it is," I agree brightly, a tingling sensation at the base of my neck urging me forward.

We slowly and carefully maneuver through the vegetation, taking deliberate steps to avoid treading on the extraordinary, glowy flowers, hardly making a sound.

My senses feel heightened, the music from the beach party having long since faded away. There is a strange stillness to the forest, as if it's lying in wait for something to happen.

"Cece, does this feel weird to you?" I whisper so softly I doubt she can hear me.

"The air feels charged, like right before a storm. It's got the hairs on the back of my neck standing up," Cece whispers back, voice equally soft.

"Be careful, okay?"

"You too."

Cece and I fall silent again, as do our surroundings, and that eerie feeling grows thicker.

I lead the way with an ever-growing sense of urgency guiding my steps through the darkening forest, following the flowers through the dense foliage.

For a moment, the stillness makes me uneasy, and I almost consider turning back, but that invisible magnetic pull compels me toward the center of the island. Cece follows closely behind, raised skirt in hand as she lightly pads across the forest floor.

We reach a small clearing and pause in front of a natural curtain of leaves overlapping each other. The flowers' trail disappears behind it.

The air feels thickest here, yet the humidity hasn't increased.

I take a deep breath and reach my hand out to Cece. Wordlessly, she clasps her hand with mine.

The curiosity to see what's on the other side of it, where the flowers have disappeared, is gnawing at me.

I nod and, just like when we were younger, she counts us down, silently mouthing the words...

Three...

Two...

One...

We each reach out a free hand and cautiously part the foliage, our knuckles turning white where we grip each other tighter.

My body locks up, momentarily stunned by what we're seeing. Hearing.

A wave of sounds—of deep masculine voices chatting, the

rushing of a waterfall, sounds of splashing, rumbling laughter—washes over me.

I blink, sure I must be mistaken. I blink again, tempted to rub at my eyes as I process what I'm seeing.

Men, but not.

Horns. Tails. Wings. Fur.

Monsters.

Monsters of all kinds hanging out in a clearing in the forest, resting on the rocks surrounding the most picturesque waterfall, jumping into the pool below.

My body sways slightly as I take it all in.

I give Cece's hand two quick, successive squeezes, checking if she's also seeing what I'm seeing.

She squeezes back once.

My heart is thumping wildly, my lungs refusing to cooperate.

As one, we slowly take a step back—sisterly telepathy thankfully still intact—hoping to disappear back into the thick forest. Pretty flowers forgotten.

Slowly, we lower the curtain of leaves back into place, but I look up and make eye contact with striking jade-green eyes. On the other side of the clearing is the most attractive man I've ever laid eyes on. Espresso-brown hair, fit body, chiseled jaw...

His eyes widen for a fraction of a second before the foliage obscures him from my sight.

I turn, ready to run, blindly grabbing for my sister's hand again. I peek over my shoulder, only to find the leaves swaying in the breeze, all sounds perfectly ensconced behind the wall of foliage once again.

As I take a step forward, with every intention of sprinting back to the beach, I whip my head back around and run straight into a rock-hard chest.

An "oof" escapes me, and I lift my free hand to inspect my nose. I look up into the piercing jade-green eyes that were just across the clearing.

He's leaning with an arm against a tree trunk like he's been here all along, looking like a model posing for a luxury brand.

A smirk tugs at the right corner of his mouth as he holds my gaze and leans forward into my personal space, pure arrogance radiating off him in palpable waves.

His tongue peeks out to wet his lips.

Are those fangs?

With a sultry baritone, he says, "Now what do we have here?"

Everett

I have no idea how these women were able to find us. The wards should be strong enough for no humans to *want* to step foot on the island, never mind walking right up to us.

I stare down into the most mesmerizing electric-blue eyes I've ever come across. "Now, what do we have here?" I can't help the smirk that quirks my lips as I lean into her space.

The moment I spotted the beauty, I put on a burst of speed and rushed to intercept them before they could disappear. I'm going to have to present them to Bertie, but I think I'll take my time. I'm not quite ready to share my discovery.

"Uh, two women who have clearly taken a wrong turn and will be going now," the pretty creature in the pink dress says, giving me a little finger wave.

She's positively exquisite, and I'd like nothing more than to get to know her—in every sense of the word. But that'll have to wait.

Interrogation first, flirting second.

I look over their shoulders to check that the curtain of leaves is in place again, shielding them from the others. With their similar features, I'm guessing the two women must be sisters, and I'm feeling oddly protective of them. I'm curious to find out why.

Focusing on the confident stunner with the heart-shaped face, I relax my shoulders and angle my head in a bid to look unaffected. "Not quite yet," I drawl. "Do tell, how did you fine ladies manage to stumble upon this island?" I lean in, picking up a tantalizing scent I can't quite place. "And not just any island... a private island." Knowing they saw my friends and me in our natural state, I tack on, "For monsters." There's no point in denying it. It takes effort to keep the mild panic, bubbling below the surface, off my face.

Pink-dress beauty looks up at me with what I suspect to be nerves, but just as quickly, a cocky mask slips into place as she quirks a brow right back at me.

"Monsters? What monsters?" she dares to ask, popping a hip and twirling a piece of hair around her finger.

She's got herself some lady balls.

Strike me now, Cupid, I think I might have found the one.

"Cute." I wink at her but then quickly school my features because I shouldn't be flirting at this moment.

This is a pressing matter. We have mere moments before the others will realize something is wrong, if they haven't done so already.

I stand a bit straighter, my brow wrinkling as I try to make sense of the situation. "Seriously though, you shouldn't have been able to find us. I'm sincerely asking you before one of the others comes out here, potentially scaring your panties off." Oh fuck, now I'm thinking of her panties. "It would be in your best interest to tell me the truth. Right now," I implore her.

My fingers stretch out toward her, the need to touch her impossible to resist. I catch myself in time, though, and fold my fingers back, securely placing my hand in my pocket.

I can almost believe that it's purely accidental that they just turned up in the clearing. Only having caught her eye for a split second before she left, I can't be sure how long they stood there, watching us. Not one of us wearing our glamour rings.

The rest of the guys are bound to notice that I zoomed off without a word and will likely come looking for me. But I want to see if I can charm some information from the ladies in an unintimidating manner before the bigger, scarier-looking guys arrive.

"Well..." The sister in the flowy dress starts.

Looking at each other, they do some kind of weird eye-communication thing. My pretty lady bites her bottom lip and nods a couple of times. They seem to have come to an agreement.

"You see..." she continues and then hesitates.

Holy fuck, if this woman doesn't get to the point, I'm going to lose it. I gesture with my hand for her to hurry it along.

My pink woman holds up her index finger and points it accusingly at me. "Excuse you, that's a bit rude, don't you think? Give me a fucking minute to collect my thoughts. You can just stand over there, looking all sexy and smug and shit. I'll tell you *what* I want to tell you *when* I want to tell you. Got that?" She punctuates the last two words with two pokes to my chest.

"You think I'm sexy," I say more than ask. A sly grin crawls across my face as I trail my gaze down her body to her sparkly pink toenails and back up again to those enchanting blue pools. "Feeling's mutual, sparkles."

The blush that tinges her cheeks shows me I've definitely struck a chord, but I'm not so sure if it's from pleasure or indignation. That's not something I should think on for too long, because just looking at her, I can only imagine how many other ways I can make her blush.

She blinks a few times as if snapping herself back to the moment. "We're leaving now. Our friends are waiting for us. We saw nothing. We'll say nothing. Thank you and goodbye."

She attempts to take a step around me, but I can't allow that quite yet.

"Hold up, sparkles." I reach out and lightly grab her wrist.

My skin touches hers, and a force of heat bursts from my

center, rolling through me in a wave. A tremor works its way from my hand up my arm, rippling down through my chest, my gut, *my cock*, and finally dissipating around my feet.

I drop her wrist.

"Did you feel that?" I ask breathlessly as I scan my body, turning my arms this way and that.

Sparkles's voice is a soft whisper as she answers, "Yes."

She looks just as confused as she inspects her wrist.

"Dede, what was that?" her sister asks, placing a comforting hand on her shoulder.

She remains speechless as she cradles her wrist.

"Sadie, are you okay?" her sister asks again, worry biting into her tone.

Sadie. It suits her.

"I'm okay. Just confused. That was super weird," she says in a small voice, very unlike the fiery woman from a moment ago.

This version of her is tugging at all my baser instincts to *protect, protect, protect.*

"All right, ladies. Something is obviously going on here. I can't allow you to leave after what you've witnessed and after that zap thing just happened. Let me call my friend whose family owns this island. Perhaps he has a very simple explanation for thi—"

"You've got to be fucking kidding me," Sadie interrupts me. "'Can't allow'? We're leaving, and there's nothing you can do about it." All the strength she momentarily lost comes back and pours steel into her voice.

It's hot.

She's a force to be reckoned with, and I'm sure some men have tried, and failed, to claim her. To tame her. A woman like Sadie needs to be appreciated and allowed to shine however brightly she fucking wants to. Most men aren't okay with being a supporting act, but for her, I'm enticed to be just that.

4

Sadie

I make to push past the insufferably attractive man, only for the world around me to blur as he whips his arm out and shoves me behind him. The action so fast that my hand slips from Cece's. Emerging from the clearing behind the curtain of foliage is a new face—strikingly beautiful in an otherworldly sense—attached to a tall frame and a mop of platinum-blond hair, which I would like to use as inspiration the next time I go for highlights. He exudes power. Or is it actual magic? I wouldn't be surprised at this point.

I shrink back, letting the green-eyed man's broad back partially hide me from the view of the newcomer. Why I feel safe with him is a mystery I'll unravel later.

It's only then that I realize Cece is standing, unprotected and alone, in front of the new guy. She doesn't look intimidated by him though, more... fascinated as they take each other in.

"Everett, who are these women?" newcomer guy with the light gray eyes asks attractive guy with the striking green eyes.

Everett, mmm, I like that.

"I was just coming to get you to figure out how they were able to penetrate the wards. I've been trying to get some answers out of them, but they're not being particularly cooperative." Everett aims a loaded look toward me over his shoulder.

"We were merely following the flowers."

Cece decides to enter the chat with that? Now they're going to think we're crazy.

At her pronouncement, the men look around and see the trail of flowers leading back the way we came. The newcomer guy goes preternaturally still and cocks his head to the side, causing his hair to slip behind his ear. His very pointy ear.

I suck in an audible breath, and everyone stares at me.

Peeking out from behind Everett's back, I aim a harsh whisper at the newcomer. "Are you like a faerie or something?" My eyes go wide as the words start spilling from me. "There were other men too. Creatures? Supernatural beings? Was that a minotaur that I saw? I could've sworn I saw a mermaid—merman? And this guy here, he's super fast. Did you know how fast he can move?"

The look on the newcomer's face brings my babbling to a screeching halt. I put both my hands up, realizing I've gone on too long. The shock of what I saw must have momentarily shorted my brain and any self-preservation instincts I have.

Partially moving back behind Everett again, my shoulders draw up high as I say, "But I promise you, we won't say anything. Seriously. We'll just be on our way and—"

"Enough!" maybe-faerie guy cuts me off. "I can sense that there are other humans on this island. I have no idea how that is possible, but we cannot allow you to leave until we have the answers as to how you were able to sneak this far onto the island. Especially without me detecting it." He attempts to soften his expression. "We mean you no harm. But since we are unsure of what forces are at play here, it is for your own safety that I request you and your companions come with us up to the manor, and then I'll answer *some* of your questions."

"How can you 'sense' the others?" I throw at him, fingers in obnoxious quotation marks as I step out from behind Everett. "If only my sister and I saw you, don't you have to be concerned about only us? The others don't even know anything."

"The 'others' are actually headed this way as we speak." Everett points in the general direction from which we came.

I turn and crane my neck but don't see anything through the trees. "I can't see anything."

"I can hear them approaching. They're quite... rowdy. Sounds like a fun party," Everett tacks on, nodding as if in approval.

"More like an assault to the senses," newcomer guy adds.

Ugh, this guy screams buzzkill.

Ignoring him, Everett cocks his head. Biting his lip with an elongated canine, he gives me a quick once-over and says in a low voice, "But you, you're the MVP of the party, aren't you?" He winks.

Holy shit. Why is that so hot?

"There you are! We were wondering where you ran off to," Iris shouts in relief, leading the group of girls.

They all move within hearing distance—human hearing anyway—but keep a safe distance from us and the men.

"Who are these guys?" Helena asks, clearly wary of any men after her recent experiences.

Newcomer steps forward and places a hand on his chest. "Ladies, please allow me to introduce myself. My name is Adelbert Alberad. My family owns this island and, by proxy, I am therefore responsible for your safety. It has come to our attention that you have inadvertently breached our security measures, and I would like to ascertain how that may have come about. If you would be so kind as to follow me up to the manor, then we can discuss this matter further, and possibly alleviate any concerns you might have."

Dead silence follows his eloquent spiel. Then, raucous laughter.

"The balls on this guy!"

"Did he just...?"

"I mean..."

The girls are all talking over each other, but the sentiment is the same. None of us are following this guy anywhere.

The moment the noise tapers down to a more normal level,

the curtain of leaves parts, and a set of curved horns bursts through. Then another set of horns on a being with extended wings appears. Different types of monsters keep coming through until everyone is gathered on our side of the clearing.

One of the women screams. Most, though, are stunned into silence as their eyes stay riveted to the scene. Hands shoot to cover mouths, one or two of the women take a step back, but Natalie quirks her head, giving a certain set of horns a curious perusal.

Everett places himself in front of me again, partially blocking me from the monsters' view.

When everyone freezes, he turns his head and whispers to me, "Oh, fuck. Shit just got interesting, don't you think, sparkles?"

Everett

My friends smash through the barrier, their boisterous mood propelling them forward. I instinctively step in front of Sadie in an effort to protect her—from what, I'm not quite sure. My friends might look intimidating, but they're really kind guys.

When they catch sight of the human females, they immediately come to a halt. The sight of their brows shooting up into their hairlines and jaws practically hitting the floor brings me a peculiar sense of enjoyment.

The females quiet down instantly. A tense stare-down commences with no one bold enough to make a move quite yet, each too nervous to startle the other.

Two opposing groups of roughly similar numbers, except vastly different in size and species, squaring off—nothing weird about that.

"Now it looks like a party," I say loudly into the clearing, attempting to break the ice.

Sadie turns to me and whispers, "If I pinkie promise I won't say anything, can I just like… go?"

Oh, sweet Sadie, if only you were so lucky. Bertie's in charge here, and that means he's probably concocted a plan already and has two contingency plans ready to go. None of them would include turning away and pretending this didn't happen.

Bertie steps forward, hands up and palms facing outward—the universal sign for "I come in peace"—and addresses the women first.

"I apologize for the abrupt appearance of my brethren. Please do not fret. Though their monstrous appearance may startle you at first glance, I can assure you they mean you no harm. I can attest to the sound character of each."

I wish he didn't sound like he was in the middle of a council meeting with a bunch of elves with carrots shoved up their butts—and not in the fun way. He might be scaring the women more with his fancy speech than Harvey's or Jasper's horns are.

I try to smooth things over. "Ladies, what my dear friend Bertie is trying to say is that we're all cool, despite some looking like monsters. Which we are, but I promise you're safe with us. I think we just need to figure out how you were able to get on the island when there were things in place to deter you," I calmly translate into normal speak.

I look over to Bertie, and he confirms with a stiff nod. With the solemn set to his mouth and his hands clasped behind his back, he's unintentionally doing a fine imitation of his father.

"Boys, how about heading up to the house ahead of the ladies? Put on some dry clothes, don your rings, and prepare some refreshments. Bertie and I can escort the ladies," I tell the others, imploring them with my eyes to be cool and not freak the women out any more than they already have.

"You heard him, guys. Let's get going," Edmond encourages in an unperturbed tone, practically herding them with his massive stone arms spread wide, tail flicking behind him, belying his calm acceptance of the situation.

I can appreciate that he tucked his wings closer to his body from their full spread once he realized there was no threat.

While the guys make their exit, my eyes can't help but

draw back to Sadie. I wonder what she's making of all my friends. Is she scared of them? *Attracted to them?* The thought is like a fist right to my solar plexus.

I stick my elbow out toward Sadie and incline my head. "Milady."

She furrows her brows, eyes darting about, then tentatively reaches out a hand and places it in the crook of my elbow.

"This is weird. I don't know what's happening, but I'm just going to say fuck it and hope for the best. You better not be in some type of cult or murder me," she adds in a completely flat tone.

"It disturbs me that murder was second in that sentence. But I can vow that no murdering will be happening tonight."

Sadie stares up at me, searching for something in my face. I try to meet her eyes with all the sincerity that I feel.

Apparently happy with what she finds, she shrugs, glances over her shoulder, and calls, "Okay, ladies, let's move the party up to the house. No murders on the horizon."

Miraculously, they decide to follow us, and Bertie's shoulders sag in relief. He gestures for Sadie's sister to walk in front of him. The two exchange some light pleasantries in hushed tones. I'd consider listening in, but I'd much rather focus my attention on the beautiful woman I'm escorting.

"So, how do you ladies all know each other?" I ask Sadie, hoping to use the walk to get to know her better.

She chuckles. "Would you believe that we've only known each other a couple of hours? We met Iris and Helena earlier this week, and they invited us along for a sunset cruise. We only met the other girls tonight. Would not have predicted our night ending up like this."

"Wow, you guys really didn't mean to end up here, did you?"

I'll definitely have to tell Bertie how accidental their arrival actually was. No way they could've orchestrated such an elaborate scheme to find us when they've only just met.

Sadie purses her lips and shakes her head slowly. "Nope.

An island full of monsters was not on my bingo card for the night."

"And what was?" I goad her, letting her see the mischief on my face before I turn back to watch the path.

Sadie's voice is thick with innuendo as she looks up at me with a smirk that makes my knees weak. "Well, there's this one thing— Nope. I have so many filthy responses, but I'm going to keep it clean. For now."

My lips turn down in mock disappointment but I let the comment slide in favor of getting to know her better.

She continues in a more thoughtful tone, "How about you guys? Monsters on a private island in the Caribbean, how did that happen?"

"This island is owned by Bertie's family and was warded specifically for our reunion this weekend. We haven't all been together like this since we graduated." I grin at how happy I am to see my friends in one place after so long.

All the guys went their separate ways after school, moving back to their home countries, taking over family businesses or starting new ones. Many of them are bound to legacy positions and don't have much choice in their futures, it's all dictated by the fates, our families, and our species.

Sadie's eyes brighten with curiosity, her whole being perking up as she looks up at me. "Where did you go to school? Is it like a secret monster school?" she adds in an excited whisper.

"It's called Alberad School for the Supernatural. We usually have meetups there since the grounds are warded and concealment is guaranteed. It's enshrouded deep in the Black Forest, hundreds of years of continuous warding keeping humans from accidentally stumbling upon it." I give her a pointed look as I help her step over a log.

The curriculum provides a perfect environment to learn control of our powers. It encourages the exploration of individual abilities while providing support and guidance from the highly knowledgeable elves and their extensive library on the premises.

"Then why didn't you just go there?" Sadie asks, her brows drawing together in confusion.

I shrug because the answer seems so selfish now. "We wanted a real vacation, on a beach. This island was here, so it only made sense to enjoy it. All of us monsters carry some magic around with us and it tends to mess with the natural order of things if there's a larger group of us gathering outside of any wards. Bertie said his father came with some other elves to coordinate the whole warding process, ensuring the highest safety standards for the reunion."

Sadie scoffs. "Apparently Bertie's father and the elves weren't very successful."

Shaking my head profusely, I say, "You don't get it. Bertie's family runs the school. They study magic every day. If they warded this place, it shouldn't be able to be found. I don't think this has happened before. That's why I'm worried, Bertie even more so."

Realization dawns on her face. "Oh shit. So this isn't the case of someone simply fucking up?"

"I don't know. That's why we're going to the manor, to see if we can chat it through and figure out how it was possible. You guys shouldn't have even been able to get *on* the island, never mind venturing so far inland and finding us," I explain, already racking my brain for possible ways this could have happened.

I decide to go into more detail so she can understand how significant them finding us is. "The wards grow incrementally stronger the closer to the manor we get. Bertie said the entire island has a repulsion charm placed around it. Then, there's a sound ward, which extends to the curtain of leaves you saw us through at the waterfall. And finally, the strongest wards are placed around the main property, shielding the manor from view. They're spelled to make it look like an uninhabited island."

Sadie blinks a couple of times at the new information, then nods slowly in understanding. "The strong reactions from Bertie and the others are starting to make more sense now."

I take a moment to study her profile, lingering on her

luscious lips—so pink, almost like they're begging to be nibbled on. She catches me staring, and I feel a rare blush heating my cheeks. I suck my lip between my teeth and worry at it, a sad replacement for hers.

Trying to draw attention away from myself, I say, "You're handling all this surprisingly well."

Sadie lifts her shoulders in a shrug. "I'm just embracing my new 'fuck-it' attitude."

Oh shit, I'm in trouble. I wish that "fuck-it attitude" includes me.

I swallow hard and focus on my steps, hoping to redirect my impure thoughts.

Her attention turns to Bertie and her sister walking ahead of us. Bertie's leaning his head slightly toward the woman, listening intently to what she's saying.

Bending down and putting my mouth closer to Sadie's ear than strictly necessary, I say in a low voice, "I think Bertie might have a little crush. Is your sister single?"

Sadie stops walking and whips her head around to glare up at me, unwittingly putting our mouths a mere breath apart. For a moment, time stops. We lock eyes and just breathe each other in. Until I, like the idiot I am, clear my throat.

She retreats and faces forward again, almost stumbling over her feet on her next step. I automatically flex my arm where her hand rests, hoping it stabilizes her without being too obvious about it.

"Leave Florence alone. She's too good for Bertie," she says vehemently.

"I have no doubt about that," I agree. "But FYI, I think if you call my friend 'Bertie' to his face, you might just give him hemorrhoids. That nickname has been earned from being roommates at boarding school since the age of ten."

"So, I'm supposed to call him what?" She arches an imperious brow.

"Adelbert. His full name. He's very… particular about it," I reply carefully.

I bend down again to place my mouth close to her ear. Allowing my lips to skim the shell, I whisper, "But you can call *me* anything you like."

A full-body shudder works its way down from her shoulders. With my enhanced eyesight, I can make out the goose bumps that dot her arms in the evening's dimming light. Hoping her reaction is not a sign of revulsion, I surreptitiously scent the air. I get the barest hint of her blooming arousal and mentally high-five my flirting skills.

Realizing that if I can scent her, the other guys can too, I decide to cease my flirting. For the time being, anyway.

She scoffs. "How about 'no thanks?'"

"Oh no, you don't, sparkles. I know you can do better than that," I cajole.

"Let's just stick to names. I'm Sadie. That's my sister Florence. I heard Adelbert call you Everett. Is that right?"

"Fair enough. But I think I'll stick to sparkles," I add with a crooked smile, mirth evident in my voice.

"If you get to give me a nickname, then I'm going to pick one for you too. Just you wait," she throws back at me, briefly looking up at me through squinted eyes, before fixing her gaze on her feet again as she carefully navigates the forest floor.

If she only knew me, she'd trust that I wouldn't let her hurt so much as her little toe. I've been keeping a keen eye out on every bit of the path where she's had to place her feet since we started our walk.

Appearing marginally unsure of herself, she asks, "In the meantime, can I ask you a question?"

I raise an expectant brow, silently prodding her to continue.

Sadie twirls a strand of hair around her finger. "I don't want to sound rude, and I don't know what the proper customs are, and I don't want to overstep. So just tell me to shut up if—"

"You want to know what kind of monster I am," I surmise.

"Well... yeah." Her grin is sheepish, her nose adorably scrunched up.

"All in good time, sparkles. We have arrived at our destination," I tack on, imitating a GPS device.

6

Sadie

By the time we arrive at the stately manor, the sky is a deep blue with only traces of pinks and purples remaining, as the first stars wink at us.

"Wow." I come to a complete stop as I stare up at the multistory limestone house with its tall columns and arched doorways.

Nestled into the natural slope of the mountain, it takes advantage of the incline by spreading out across four separate buildings, centered around the larger main house.

I can only imagine the majestic ocean views each room must give its occupants from this height. Perhaps a tad more grandiose than our budget-friendly hotel.

Resuming walking, we pad up the wide stone stairs with hushed voices, a sense of awe descending on us as Adelbert leads us to the "great room," where a group of men are standing around, quietly talking among themselves.

The large, high-ceilinged room screams old money with its cream color palette, tufted white couches, and gold accents in the dimmed lighting fixtures artfully placed throughout. Tall glass folding doors that open onto a deck overlooking an infinity pool and the dark sea beyond, take up an entire wall.

Adelbert steps into the middle of the room and addresses

us. "Ladies, please have a seat."

Belatedly, I find my hand is still in the crook of Everett's elbow. I go to pull it free, but Everett traps it with a squeeze of his arm. I glare at him as the corner of his mouth curls up in a wicked grin. He winks and loosens his grip before swaggering over to join the men.

I swear, the winks are going to drive me mad. I refuse to acknowledge their effect on the gusset of my panties, though.

The women huddle together on the tufted velvet couches on the left of the room.

"Saved you a seat," Natalie calls, patting the spot on the other side of her and Diana, scooching over so Cece and I can join them.

Absently, I run my fingers over the soft velvet as my gaze keeps flicking to Everett. One of the men hands him something and then gives one to Adelbert too.

I narrow my eyes in concentration, and my lips quirk when I see they're putting on rings. All the men are now wearing matching rings. Studying them, I realize they resemble the monsters from the forest, but they look like normal human men... Okay, normal, very attractive human men.

I recall what Everett said earlier and take a guess that magic is involved because that one guy who totally had wings earlier no longer does. And the guy with the horns, who had Natalie curious, is leaning casually on a jutted hip, looking completely normal, if not still a bit imposing.

When Adelbert moves to the center of the room, I snap my mouth closed, scared I was caught staring. I take a deep breath in through my nose and relax my shoulders on the exhale, in a bid to look calmer than I feel.

Taking on a formal stance with hands clasped in front of his body, Adelbert addresses the room. "Welcome to the Alberad Caribbean Estate. I shall get straight to the point. Your presence on this island is highly disturbing to me. It defies all the laws of our magic. This residence has been in my family for many generations, and our wards have never been breached. The supernatural beings of the world prefer to keep our existence concealed." His gaze drops to the floor, and his voice deepens. "Humans are... unpredictable at best."

Lifting his head, Adelbert looks back at us, his brows drawn tight and lips in a hard, flat line. With a sudden dry mouth, I swallow the bundle of nervous energy that's telling me I'm in the presence of a powerful being... a room full of monsters parading as humans. Cece reaches for my hand, a comforting presence easing my nerves some.

Wiping the intensity from his eyes, Adelbert lets a tight smile curve his lips as he says, "Our secrecy is both for your benefit as well as ours. It is, therefore, imperative that we determine how you were able to make landfall upon this island. Until this is concluded, I must insist you all remain here... as my guests, of course."

Everett stands abruptly and joins Adelbert. His posture is a clear juxtaposition with his palms open and raised. "What he's trying to say is monsters are real, such as yours truly." He holds his index finger up, the green gem on his ring glinting in the soft light. "We use these enchanted rings to glamour our physical natures. They help us appear human and blend into society... if we so choose. Everyone following so far?" Everett speeds through the explanation.

This is all so surreal, yet I can't help the flutter of excitement in my stomach. Magic. Monsters. The women on my couch nod easily to Everett's question, but my glance around the room catches some of my other companions looking a little green.

Everett smiles and lets his eyes rest on me for a second before he goes on, "Good. Bertie over here, is an elf. You may have seen his pointy ears? Well, pointy before he put his glamour ring on. His family is in charge of the school for the supernatural that we attended together from the age of ten. That's how we all met.

It's a boarding school in the Black Forest. This weekend is our ten-year reunion. All of us lived in the same wing for eight years." He pauses, taking time to look at each of us. "You still with me?"

More nods, slightly more lively this time around.

Everett holds my gaze a little longer this time, a ghost of a smile twitching his lips. I bite my answering smile back as he shifts his gaze to the rest of the room and continues, "Bertie's family also owns this island. It has a bunch of magic and spells deterring humans from accessing it." A slight frown mars his brow. "Somehow, you were able to bypass all security measures and evade detection from supernatural beings with highly attuned senses. We want to know how or why that happened."

Everett's eyes return to me, and my cheeks heat as his tongue runs over a long canine.

After a tense moment, he grins, turning to Adelbert. "Does that about sum up what you want to say, Bertie?"

Adelbert tugs on the back of his neck, his lips pressing into a tight line before he calmly says, "Thank you, Everett. That shall suffice."

Pressing her palms to the velvet cushion, Iris scoots forward, drawing the attention of everyone in the room as she says, "One: we had no idea this was a private island. I chartered that boat, its captain brought us here. Maybe interrogate him. And two: speaking of the captain, it's late and he's probably waiting, so we should get going now."

I take in her confident posture and clear voice. Iris is the badass boss I can only aspire to be.

Adelbert shakes his head. "I am afraid that is out of the question. I shall send someone to communicate your change of plans to the captain of your boat."

I don't think he was hugged much as a child. He needs some TLC or someone to smooth his very pointy edges. Maybe give him some head scratches.

From the corner of my eye, I catch my sister staring at

him as if transfixed, and not for the first time tonight. *Hmm.*

Helena crosses her arms, asking, "Remain with you as guests or as prisoners?"

Oh no, no man is safe around a woman scorned.

Hide your balls, boys.

Adelbert scrubs a hand through his pretty platinum hair, possibly not aware that he's making himself look more disheveled with each pass. It's oddly humanizing.

When he opens his mouth, his voice has a pleading note to it. "We mean you no harm. I vow by the fates that you are safe in this house with us." He takes turns to look each of us in the eyes.

Cece lifts a hand to draw Adelbert's attention. Ever intuitive and adept at minimizing confrontation, she says in a gentle tone, "Maybe you can tell us a little about yourselves? I think that will help everyone feel more comfortable."

Adelbert looks at Cece with so much gratitude, a soft smile pulling at the corners of his mouth, head nodding furiously, somewhat out of character from what I've seen of him so far.

"That is a splendid notion, Florence."

He makes quick work of introducing each of the males, which we learn is what they prefer to be called, and sharing what type of supernatural being they are. He also adds that they do refer to themselves as monsters and have no qualms about us using the same term if we wish.

There is a minotaur, a gargoyle, a selkie, a grim reaper, a krampus, a leprechaun, and even a couple of shifters.

When it's Everett's turn to introduce himself, I find myself sitting up a bit straighter in my seat, subconsciously smoothing out the nonexistent creases in my skirt.

"Once again, I'm Everett. I'm a dhampir—Dad's a vampire, Mom's a human. Got the benefit of the heightened senses and speed of a vampire but the lifespan of a human. Also, most notably, I don't drink blood. But I do have these." He bares his teeth and looks over at me as he slides his tongue over a sharp canine.

It's not entirely giving me vampire vibes, but there is most definitely a sense of "other."

If he doesn't drink blood, I can't help but wonder what those sharp teeth are for.

I'm suddenly hit with a picture of me bent over in front of a mirror, him fucking into me from behind, with his teeth—fangs?—glinting as he fixes his eyes on my neck, a ravenous look on his face.

Panties: flooded. Hope this manor has a mop.

Also, him being a dhampir totally explains how he got from the other side of the clearing so fast. I'm kind of curious about what his heightened senses could pick up, but not like I'm going to be asking him.

Wait... can he... smell me? The effect he has on my underwear?

I'm pulled from my thoughts as Iris waves her phone around and says, "Thank you for sharing all of that. I think I can speak for all the girls in saying I feel marginally better about being here. But someone does need to contact our captain because none of us have any signal."

Adelbert's throat bobs on a swallow as he scratches at the back of his neck. It's almost like he's speaking to himself when he says, "At least that's working." He looks at Iris, bowing slightly. "My apologies. When the wards work correctly, the magic blocks cellular services on the island."

Jamie, the leprechaun, offers, "I'll shoot down to the beach quickly. Won't take two secs. I'll tell your cap that we'll see to your transport and he can return to the docks."

If I remember correctly from his introduction, he's able to teleport across certain distances.

He must be a fun friend to have around.

Iris accepts stiffly, "Thank you, Jamie. That's very kind of you."

Jamie winks out of existence right in front of our eyes, only to appear seconds later in the same spot, sporting a bloody nose.

Thrusting his hands on his hips, he shakes his head and grins through the blood trickling from his nose. "So, that didn't quite go according to plan. I swear, I don't usually have performance issues."

1

Sadie

The room erupts with varying reactions to Jamie's appearance. Cece sucks in an audible gasp, her face the picture of concern, hands stretched out as if wanting to help. In contrast, Iris bites down on her lips, shoulders jumping up and down as she tries to rein in her laughter.

Jamie seems stunned more than hurt as all our gazes stay riveted on him. Pink blooms across his cheeks as he lets his eyes flit about the room, avoiding making eye contact with anyone while Adelbert hovers his hands over Jamie's nose. I think he's using magic to heal him.

Iris manages to push out, "Are you okay?" before a snort escapes her.

After a second, most of the women join in and soon, the contagious laughter spreads around the room, infecting us all, even Jamie.

The ice is officially broken, just like Jamie's nose seemed to be.

As the laughter starts to taper off, Natalie points at the ink visible on her thigh, right below the hem of her pleated skirt. "So, not to alarm anyone or anything, but this is new."

I look closer at the ink. It's an intricate design of an overlaid sun, moon, and star. It's beautiful.

I look up to see Everett exchange a worried glance with Adelbert, his eyes nearly bugging out of his head.

My pulse starts racing, and I turn my gaze to the rest of the room. Everyone is inspecting their bodies. I'm too nervous to check mine.

Slowly but surely, the women begin sharing about their own fresh ink. They all seem to have the same design but in different spots on their bodies.

"I have one on my wrist," Cordelia states.

"Me too." Erik walks over to Cordelia and compares their wrists.

I think he said he's a selkie—I had mistakenly thought him a merman before.

Damn, now *they* would make a cute couple. Both are tall, blonde, and athletic, their sun-kissed skin making them look like they spend all their free time surfing.

Adelbert moves to the front of the room and raises his voice above the din.

"Could each of you be so kind as to please voice if you have discovered a new marking and said marking's location? I would like to ascertain if a counterpart could be paired."

I can't explain why, but once again my eyes travel to Everett as he scans his body, peeking down the collar of his black button-down. A lead weight drops in my stomach at the thought of him finding a matching tattoo with one of the other ladies.

Spurred on by this unexpected emotion, I double my efforts, craning my neck this way and that to scrutinize every visible inch of my body. I copy some of the other girls by getting up and looking at the backs of my legs even.

Nothing.

"Dede. There." Cece points to my right leg.

"Where?" I walk my feet apart and shift my right knee outward.

Suddenly, Everett is in front of me—on his knees—inspecting my inner thigh with his eyes only, hands hovering as if wanting to touch me but not quite daring to. Still, I can almost feel his phantom touch.

He smirks up at me and licks his lips lasciviously. "I bet next time I'm down here, it'll be for a different reason."

Before I can gather my wits to think of something snarky to reply with, he's gone, no trace of him in the room with us.

Good thing too, because he's not wrong.

I look at the symbols on my inner thigh. "This tattoo is actually cool. I don't think I would've thought of this spot for myself, but I love it. Kind of sexy." Turning to my sister, I ask, "Cece, have you found yours?"

"Yes," she whispers, eyes darting around the room, pulling her bottom lip into her mouth.

"Where?"

Before she's able to reply, Everett has zoomed back into the room. Stalking over to me, he leans into my personal space, leveling his jade-green eyes with mine.

"Looks like we're a tattoo twosome, sparkles."

8

Everett

As soon as Florence asked Sadie about her tattoo, I had to see for myself. There's this invisible tether to her—like I'm constantly aware of where she is in a room.

It would be highly inconvenient, but she intrigues me. She's brave, witty, and unbelievably beautiful. And she has claws. I wonder what they'll feel like scratching down my back as I pin her down, drawing out screams of ecstasy...

Finding her tattoo compelled me to inspect my inner thigh. I rushed to the bathroom to check if the fates could possibly be kind enough to give me its twin.

Spoiler alert, they're the kindest.

I swear relief flashes in her eyes before she carefully covers it with a nonchalant expression and pops her hip. "Well, aren't you lucky?"

"I most certainly am." Even though I say it in a very flirty tone, I'm sincere.

There are some amazing women present in the room, but none hold a candle to Sadie.

Bertie clears his throat, the sound like splashing cold water in my face, defusing the tension between Sadie and me. "It seems that most of us have found a tattoo partner. I am unsure as to the meaning of this, but I shall head to the library to commence research pertaining to this unique predicament and find a means to dissolve the markings that have appeared. I apologize for the inconvenience. Please help yourselves to some refreshments while the males prepare your accommodations. We shall return shortly to take you to your wing. I apologize once again, but I will do my utmost to make sure you are as comfortable as possible while we figure this out."

It's clear that he isn't the one responsible for what's happening, and I hope the women can see that too. I can't help but feel sorry for him—and admire him at the same time—for taking on this burden, the same as he always takes responsibility to lead and make smart choices. Choices that don't always benefit him but would make his family proud. Though, they would never outwardly show any kind of approval to him, only note when he hasn't fully satisfied their expectations.

Guess my dear old father has that in common with Bertie's family.

Iris steps forward with hands on her hips. "Lovely speech, Adelbert. And not to knock the wind out of your sails, but before all the males leave, I would like to know what the captain said about us not returning. I hope he understood and is not sending out a search party or anything." She's clearly peeved that her earlier request has gone ignored and everyone's already being dismissed.

I'm also guilty of forgetting about the boat situation there for a second while getting caught up in discovering fancy new tattoos.

Jamie shoves his hands in his pockets and says, "Thanks, Iris. I was going to say something before everyone started laughing at the state I was in. It was warranted, though. I looked a right mess." He chuckles and subconsciously rubs at his freshly healed nose. "When I went to teleport, I smashed into a barrier of some kind. It's never happened before. Usually, if I try to go too far, I have a stretching sensation before reaching my limit. But this was just like running into a solid wall. Hence the bloody nose and sore arm."

I offer, "Bertie, let me run down to the beach real quick and see if I can find the problem."

"Thank you, Everett. That would be most kind. Everyone, let's remain gathered here until the return of—"

I zoom out of the house before he has even finished his sentence, hoping to help lessen my friend's worries, and send the captain on his way. The women will be safe with us. We'll figure this all out, and then we'll take our boat out tomorrow morning for a short cruise before dropping them off and sending them on their way.

Maybe I'll be lucky enough to get Sadie's number.

I race down the hill, eager to show off how fast I can make the return trip, and... BAM... Dull pain spears down the front of my body.

Seems Jamie was right. At least I didn't break my nose.

I guess teleporting would do that.

Sticking my hands out, I search for the barrier but can't feel anything solid. I try to take a step forward again and feel resistance against my body. The wall is definitely not solid; it almost feels like an opposing magnet repelling me.

I try to force my way through it one more time.

It's like I'm moving through mud, but I persist, managing one full step forward.

An unexpected, peculiar tugging in my gut makes me think of Sadie, urging me to return to her.

If I've learned one thing tonight, it's that the fates are up to something and I should trust them.

With that thought, I race back to the manor house. To Sadie.

Sadie

One moment, Everett was standing next to me, then he vanished. Only the stirring of a few strands of my hair was a testament to his presence and supernatural speed. I wonder if Everett will be able to convince the captain to leave us here. Somehow, I know he'll manage. That man can charm the panties off a nun.

It's highly inconvenient that I'm thinking of him so much. We just met, and I'm practically salivating at the thought of what kind of shenanigans we could get up to. The image of him on his knees in front of me earlier, but this time doing all kinds of delicious things, is playing on a loop in my brain. Imagining my fingers gripping his espresso-brown hair, one leg draped over his broad shoulder, as I direct him where to—

Suddenly, I'm off my feet and have moved a foot forward, as if pulled by a phantom hook, having no idea how that happened.

"What the fuck?" I ask no one in particular.

All the women, even the males, stand and move toward me. They're hovering just out of reach, as if afraid to touch me, talking all at once, but I'm not listening to them.

My vision tunnels, and my ears feel like they're underwater. There's a strange tugging sensation in my stomach as

I skid another foot forward.

Feeling thoroughly unmoored, I stare down at my feet like they've betrayed me. My throat constricts, my heart thumps powerfully like it's trying to beat outside of my chest.

Two familiar shoes appear in front of my treacherous feet. A gentle finger tucks under my chin, tilting my head up. Familiar jade-green eyes stare into my soul, anchoring me back into my body.

"Are you alright?" Everett asks earnestly.

Concerned eyes search my face for any discomfort, moving down the rest of my body—this time with no salacious intent—as he takes stock of me.

"I think so," I breathe out, reaching out my hand to place it on his forearm.

The effect is instantaneous. Touching him grounds me. I come back to myself and look around the room, taking note of the raised eyebrows and slack jaws on some faces, and the furrowed brows etched in confusion on others.

Everett turns to the room and places one of his hands on top of mine, where it still rests on his arm, his warm skin a comforting touch. He addresses the room. "Can everyone please take a seat? I think I've discovered something else that might complicate our situation. Actually, Jamie did earlier, but we got sidetracked."

Absolutely no one moves. It's as if his words have frozen them to the spot.

He continues, "Oookay, um"—he looks to me, and though I'm not sure what's going on, I give him an encouraging nod—"seems like the fates have another surprise for us. If I'm not mistaken, we now have a limit to the distance we can be separated from our... tattoo partner." The last part comes out as more of a question.

He's clearly unsure of what to call the weird dynamic with the tattoo pairings.

Helena unceremoniously drops onto a couch and lets out a loud "ugh."

One by one, everyone follows suit and sits down without uttering a word.

I look over at Cece as she plays with the ends of her hair. The smile she sends my way is soft and meant to be reassuring, but I know my sister. She's hiding nerves under that calm demeanor.

I wonder who her partner is—she never got around to telling me.

Adelbert is pacing, running his hand through his hair for the umpteenth time, as he mutters to himself. I do not fancy being in his position right now.

Abruptly, he ceases his pacing and turns to Jamie. "Jamie, have you deduced similar findings earlier upon teleporting?"

Jamie holds up a hand, his eyes widening slightly. "Well now, hold on a sec. I experienced a wall, as was clearly evidenced by my bloody nose, but I wouldn't go so far as to say it's connected to someone specifically. I honestly thought it was similar to the sound insulation ward you had installed around the waterfall. Like maybe you just supercharged the repulsion ward and accidentally made it a physical wall. To me, that sounds way more plausible."

I don't know anything about magic, but Jamie makes a fair point.

Adelbert, looking mightily pissed now, narrows his eyes at Jamie. "I don't make mistakes. I make careful calculations before I cast wards. In addition, it was overseen by the council, so your inference is void."

Everett clears his throat, drawing all eyes to him—us. Helena's eyes drift to my hand, and I realize it's still covered by Everett's. I go to remove it, only for Everett to firm his hold, his thumb continuing to absentmindedly trace patterns on my skin. Weirdly, I don't mind it, despite the disapproval radiating off Helena.

Everett's calm voice carries around the room. "My

deduction was made because when I reached that limit, not only did I feel the invisible barrier, but also an urging sensation in my gut, a clear call to return to Sadie over here." He briefly applies pressure to my hand again as he gestures with his head toward me.

I look up at him, a blush coloring my cheeks, warmth stealing up my body.

With laughter apparent in his voice, Jasper says, "Are you sure the sensation wasn't lower than your gut, Everett? No one will blame you. Sadie's looking very scrumptious."

A giggle escapes from Natalie, but she quickly covers her mouth with both her hands.

"Watch your fucking mouth when talking about her," Everett grits out, index finger pointing threateningly at Jasper.

Jasper raises his hands in mock surrender. "I was merely kidding. Sorry, Sadie. I meant no offense. You're beautiful, and Everett has clearly noticed that."

Sylvia is watching the exchange with wide eyes, her hand clasped against the base of her throat as her eyes flit between the males.

Trying to de-escalate the situation, I decide to step in. "Um, thanks, I guess. And don't worry, I've clearly noted how pretty Everett is too," I add, patting Everett's shoulder with my free hand. To the room, I say, "Everett wasn't the only one who felt that. You guys all saw me be basically propelled across the room, my body moving of its own accord. I have no idea how that happened, but how Everett explained it is exactly how it felt for me too."

Jamie asks, "But why would you two feel a pull to each other? I simply felt like I ran into a wall, no urging or calling whatsoever. Though I did spare a thought for pretty Iris over there." He waggles his eyebrows at Iris.

Iris scoffs and rolls her eyes. "I always like being a man's 'spare thought.' You know just how to make a girl feel special, Jamie. I'm practically melting into a puddle over here." Sarcasm drips from every word, her hand pressed to her chest in a mock swoon.

Adelbert runs a hand through his hair and tugs at it. "Is there any reason you can think of that things would be different with you and Sadie? Something you've done?"

Diana leans forward, Alice also turning in her seat, waiting to hear Everett's answer.

Under his breath, Everett mumbles, "There are lots of things I'd *like* to do with Sadie." His proclamation makes me squirm. Raising his voice so the rest of the room can hear him, he says, "I don't know if this could be it, but we have physically touched. When I grabbed her wrist back in the forest and touched her skin for the first time, it was like a jolt went through my body. She felt something too." He looks at me for confirmation, and I nod assertively, giving him a faint smile. "I think we got distracted by more pressing matters, and it didn't occur to me to revisit that moment until now."

"Oh yeah, Iris and I haven't touched... yet." Jamie's boldness as he throws her an exaggerated wink makes me giggle.

Iris is in for a hell of a ride if she's linked to that leprechaun.

Adelbert looks around the room. "Has any male here made physical contact with one of the women, except for Everett and Sadie?"

Sawyer stands in the corner with his arms crossed over his chest. He shakes his head as he stares at Louisa. My eyes bounce to her as she mirrors his stance, crossing her arms and leaning back on the couch.

Adelbert moves his gaze to each of the males in turn as they, too, shake their heads.

When he reaches Jasper, the krampus bites his lip, looking over at Natalie, and says, "Not yet."

Natalie shrugs one shoulder back at him, the smirk on her lips evident she wouldn't mind his touch.

Adelbert rubs at his brow. "How far would you estimate

this distance limit to be, Everett?"

"I'd say about a hundred yards."

A low whistle from Rollo accompanies this declaration, along with a headshake from Erik.

Helena huffs, but I catch a bit of panic in her voice as she says, "So what you're telling us is that we now have a hundred-yard limit from the matchy tattoo?"

Adelbert lets out a long-suffering sigh, his shoulders drooping as he says, "It would seem that we can conclude that, yes. The fates have presumably intended for us to meet and orchestrated some of tonight's events, placing various obstacles in our way to dissuade our separation. I shall promptly start my research to find the means to sever these connections as fast as the fates would allow. Please refrain from making any physical contact with your partner unless you also wish to be in a similar predicament as Everett and Sadie. I hope to have found a resolution by morning."

Adelbert's words hit me square in my chest. My fingers curl into Everett's arm.

Do I want this connection broken? Yes. Of course I do. Right?

Cece's hands pause playing with her hair, and she says, "Thank you for your hospitality. Is there anything we can do to help you with your research?"

"No, thank you. It would be most convenient for everyone to get settled for the evening. Ladies, please help yourself to some refreshments in the dining room before retiring to the east wing. If you need anything, please don't hesitate to ask one of the males, or you could approach me in the library on the second floor of the main building. Once again, please refrain from making any physical contact for the time being."

"Excuse me, Bert. If I may make a suggestion?" Harvey steps forward, hand raised patiently for permission to continue.

He's still very large in his human form, built like a

linebacker, but without his bull horns, he doesn't seem as formidable—gentle even.

"Go ahead, please." Adelbert gestures to the room, giving Harvey the floor.

"While the women look undoubtedly magnificent right now, I can suppose that their current wardrobe choices might be uncomfortable to sleep in. If we can ask the males to perhaps supply some clothing for the women, it might make them more comfortable. That is, if you are okay with sleeping in our clothing?"

A few of the women, still stuck processing the information, stare off into the distance like they don't even hear his suggestion.

Oddly, it's Helena who gives him a thumbs-up, an infinitesimal smile pulling at her mouth.

"Males, please prepare appropriate, clean clothing—no jokes, Jamie—and I will come around to your rooms to collect them. Ladies, I will deliver them to the east wing. Helena, if it is alright with you, I would like to make you the point of contact for the clothing distribution among the women." Harvey looks to Helena, waiting for confirmation.

Helena hesitates, staring at Harvey like she's caught off guard by his consideration. "Sure. Bring them to me. I'll ensure each woman gets something to sleep in."

Daehan steps forward, hands clasped behind his back. Inclining his head, he says, "Harvey, I would like to assist you with the collection."

If memory serves me, he's a grim reaper, but mostly focused on people of Korean descent who call him an angel of death. I wish I remembered more, but it was too much information and too fast for my mind to file all of their introductions away. Though, I do find that I'm remembering every single thing Everett has said.

"Thank you, Daehan. I'd appreciate your help." Harvey sounds like such a sweet-tempered giant, very thoughtful and genuine.

One by one, the ladies say their good nights and follow Edmond as he leads them to the east wing.

I grab one of Cece's hands and pull her into the far corner of the room. "You okay?"

"Sure. It's a lot of information, but everyone is trying their best to resolve it. You?"

I take a moment to think about it. "Yeah," I say, taking a deep breath before continuing. "It's definitely a lot, but I'm not getting bad vibes from anyone. I'm sure this will all blow over soon."

Cece gives me a knowing smile. "You and Everett sure seemed to hit it off."

"He's so hot, isn't he?" I whisper, fanning my face with my free hand.

"I think you two suit each other so well. I was watching you, and your chemistry is off the charts." She emphasizes the last three words.

I give a closed-mouth squeal before I say, "Yeah, his banter is great. And he's actually really nice."

Cece's eyes soften, her voice gentling as she says, "I could see that. Are you coming to bed?"

I look over at Everett, who has sprawled out on the couch—arms wrapped around the back, legs splayed arrogantly—looking way too relaxed for someone who has just been told he's magically tied to a stranger for the foreseeable future. Yet, for some reason, I'm rather reluctant to move away from him.

Looking back at Cece, I say, "In a minute. You head up first."

She squeezes my hand and gives me a wink. "See you soon, little sis. Don't do anything I wouldn't do."

As she starts walking away, I call after her, "You're only twenty-six and less than two years older than me. Don't play the big sister card now."

Cece's laughter rings out, and she gives me a wave over

her shoulder as she glides off toward the bedrooms.

Still smiling, I shift my gaze to Everett.

"So," he drawls, one brow cocked and a smirk playing along the lines of his mouth, "your room or mine?"

Everett

The look of utter indignation on Sadie's face at my proposal is priceless. I obviously didn't intend for us to room together, but she doesn't need to know that. She's just so fun to play with, and I can't resist teasing her.

I would like to officially thank the fates for their masterful plotting.

"Pft, you'd be so lucky," Sadie replies sarcastically.

"I can only hope," I shoot back, and Sadie rolls her eyes at my forwardness, an indulgent smile pulling at her lips as she sits down next to me—keeping a respectful distance.

"Not to change the topic or anything"—she raises her eyebrows—"but I'm curious about how your magic rings work." She points at the black-gold design on the index finger of my left hand.

I shift in my seat so I can face her more directly. Together we look down at the enchanted emerald at the center, glinting in the low light from the lamps scattered around the great room.

Spinning the ring with my thumb, I say, "Our glamour rings dull that sense of magic that monsters exude. They are imperative to our secrecy when living among humans. I can pass as human on an average day, even with these minor fangs that don't retract, but most of the other guys can't," I explain, thinking of Jasper in his monster form and how frightened some people might be if they met him on the street like that.

Sadie reaches out and brushes a finger over the emerald. "Do you wear it daily?"

"Yeah. It's just become a part of me now. It was gifted as a graduation present. We don't have to wear anything while at school because the wards shield us from humans. The guys took theirs off on this trip since we thought the wards would hold here too."

"Sorry, I guess?" Sadie says uncertainly, brows knitting.

I'm enjoying her company so much that when she tilts her head and scrunches her nose adorably, I shift in my seat again, readying myself for whatever question she's formulating in her mind.

She surprises me when she says, "Before I go to bed, tell me, why do you all speak so formally all the time?"

My grin is soft as I reminisce on my time spent at Alberad with the guys. "The boarding school we went to was a bit, dare I say... snobby? However, it afforded us a unique privilege—we got to be surrounded by fellow monsters from across the world. Each monster brings with them their own culture and language, on top of their individual supernatural species. This has resulted in a mélange of vocabulary and speaking styles, catalyzing the elves to teach us 'fancy' English and manners." I shrug good-naturedly. "Now, we all sound like pretentious assholes with semineutral accents, hints of each person's country peeking through at times."

"Wow. That must be a fun—and challenging—environment to grow up in," Sadie says thoughtfully.

"It was. How about you? Where do you call home?"

"Kentucky, born and bred. I'm an elementary school teacher there. What do you do?"

Not sure how much to tell her at this stage, I go with a vague answer. "I work at a hotel in Las Vegas. Ever been?"

"Not yet," Sadie purrs, giving me a look filled with trouble.

Just as quickly, the expression is gone, and she pats me on the leg. "Well, it's been quite a day. I think it's better if I'm off to bed now."

"Let me show you the way," I offer.

We both stand and walk in comfortable silence as I guide her toward the east wing. When we get to the room she's sharing with Florence, I find it difficult to say goodbye.

Remaining silent, Sadie gives me a small wave, then raps her knuckles against the door and pushes inside.

I take a last deep breath in to catch the lingering traces of her scent, closing my eyes as my olfactory receptors store the heady fragrance that is all Sadie.

Once I'm able to get my feet to move again, I hurry to my own room and pick the softest T-shirt I own—a black Loro Piana silk and cotton blend. I know it'll be big enough for her that she could wear it like a dress. The image my mind conjures of her wearing nothing but my shirt is utterly titillating. I've been painfully aware all night that she was not wearing a bra. I hope to catch a glimpse of her in that shirt in the morning, nipples pebbling against the material as the cool morning air kisses her skin.

But not wanting to come across as a total perv right off the bat, I dig out my cashmere Brunello Cucinelli sweatpants. They should be comfortable, and the drawstring will be able to tighten around her tapered waist. The fine picture her delectable ass will make in that soft charcoal... It might just be better for me not to see. I don't know if I could resist trying to take a bite.

I drop off the clothes with Daehan and head to the library to help Bertie with his research.

We have all been affected by tonight's events. There's definitely some kind of undercurrent of attraction between the males and the women. It's practically palpable if you pay attention to the signs. I feel like it's only a matter of time before things escalate between the other pairs and they join me and Sadie in the magnetic-bond club.

When I arrive in the library, all the other males are

scattered throughout, already combing through the tall shelves, fingers moving down spines as they scan titles.

The stately two-story room looks straight out of a bibliophile's fantasy. It has a jaw-dropping spiral staircase at the center, custom millwork matching the tall mahogany shelves lining the walls—stuffed to the brim with ancient and modern tomes. At the back of the room is a large, heavy desk that's some kind of Alberad family heirloom with intricate woodworking designs. This is where I find Bertie, diligently working through the stacks of books surrounding him.

"So, are we looking for anything specific, or just hoping the right book jumps out at us?" I ask Bertie.

The males close to the desk shake their heads at me, but I swear Jasper's and Jamie's lips quirk up.

"Please, no jokes right now, Everett. We are looking for all books on the fates and any mentions of unintended pairings or magical tattoos." Bertie doesn't even look up as he speaks, fully engrossed in scanning the Elvish text in front of him.

Harvey asks, "How's your Elvish, Everett? Think you can look through this section with us?" He points to a row of shelves in front of him, filled with Elvish script on the spines of timeworn tomes.

Erik confesses quietly, "I'm super rusty, haven't read one Elvish text since school."

"It's not like I read Elvish books every day either, but I'll come help." I sigh deeply as I stomp off toward them, mentally repeating the Elvish alphabet to myself to refresh my memory.

The curriculum at Alberad School for the Supernatural is very thorough. Since the school is owned and run by the elves, we learn Elvish language and history, but they also teach the general customs of fellow supernatural beings. One of our daily classes was also tailored to our individual natures, teaching us how to master control of our inherent proclivities when trying to blend into a generally human society.

Being a very rare dhampir, I was slotted in with the vampires. We had lessons concentrated on how to control our bloodlust, how to reduce a craving for blood, and even where all the best veins run in the human body and how to safely drink from them. Including guidelines on proper aftercare for a donor.

All very useful information for the vampires, but I've never so much as drooled at the sight or smell of blood, making me somewhat exempt from that particular intrinsic element.

I do, however, enjoy the benefits of the fast speed, sharp eyesight, and a keen sense of smell. They have served me particularly well in my life.

My advanced hearing tends to be a bother at times though. Like right now, when I have to listen to the grumblings of some of my friends.

"Hey, Sawyer, what's with all the huffing?" I ask my bear shifter friend.

"All the books are making me itchy, reminds me of being stuck behind a desk at school all day," Sawyer mutters grumpily.

"Missing your cabin in the woods already?"

"You guys are nice, but I need nature, man." His whole body shudders as a tremor works its way down his spine.

Harvey, ever the empath, says, "The sooner we find an answer, the sooner we'll all be back."

I smile as I recall those two during our physical education classes. I had to mentally restrain myself from running too fast during soccer, but Harvey and Sawyer—being a minotaur and bear shifter, respectively—struggled against their natural inclinations to run and bulldoze us out of the way. They were terrifying when barreling down on us, even in their glamoured forms. Thank the fates they're good guys and not typically competitive, or else we'd probably have been trampled by them.

I continue to make my way through the shelves, scanning Elvish titles, but my mind keeps drifting to Sadie. She seemed to be handling all this fairly well. Amazingly, actually. But I can't help wondering how she's really doing now that she's got some space and time to process.

I know from personal experience that in those quiet moments in the dark, surrounded by nothing but your thoughts, you're finally forced to face the things that make you uncomfortable.

She's a fascinating woman, and I don't feel like this is the end for us quite yet.

After the seventh shelf of running my fingers down spines, they stall on a title I translate to *Signs of Magic Through the Ages*. This could be something. I take it over to the desk Bertie and Edmond are at. Piles of discarded books litter the surface.

"Can I get you a whiskey, maybe? Coffee? Tea? You're looking a bit stressed," I ask Bertie quietly, even though I know everyone in the room can hear us.

"No time. Got to keep going," he says, eyes never straying from the page in front of him. "Thanks anyway."

Bertie's normally impeccably coiffed hair is looking wild with the way he's constantly running his hands through it. I wonder if this is a new nervous tic he has picked up or only due to the stress from tonight. I should probably make some time to visit him at his home in the Black Forest, which is within walking distance from Alberad—once all this has blown over, of course.

"I think I've found something here. Anyone else have any luck?" I ask, raising my voice.

"None so far. Let me see." Bertie doesn't even look up at me, just stretches out his hand and waits for me to place the book in it.

"Nothing in this one. I read the English version already." He lets out an exasperated sigh. He's even dropped his formal speech—composure slowly slipping along with his control of the situation.

"Bertie, it's okay. We'll find something. If not here, then we'll go to Alberad and search the library there."

"And how will that look? A group of human women showing up with monsters who graduated ten years ago. My father would laugh at my ineptitude."

"What other option do we have?" I ask as the other males move closer to the desk, halting their search for the time being in order to join the discussion.

"I've gone through about a hundred possibilities. Considering we have a time limit with the women having to check out of their accommodations and needing to return to their responsibilities, I've narrowed down our options to two. One really. It's a wild idea, and no one is going to like it."

"Let's hear it, then," Edmond suggests calmly.

11

Sadie

Waking up in the softest—and possibly most expensive—clothing I've ever worn to the peaceful sounds of the Caribbean jungle stirring to life around me might even be more surreal than last night. I get up from the ginormous canopied bed I shared with Cece and head to the wall of windows.

She's already awake and sitting on the balcony, curled up in a wicker bubble armchair with a light throw blanket wrapped around her shoulders. She smiles serenely up at me and inclines her head toward the other chair, which I plop down onto all too gladly. I grab another creamy throw and wrap it around my own shoulders, cuddling into the cozy cushions.

We sit in comfortable, companionable silence as we stare at the slowly lightening sky, framed by palm trees around the perimeter of the property. The lull of the ocean in the distance and the chattering of the exotic birds create the most perfect ambiance to accompany the majestic sight.

Cece is inherently an artist, and knowing how she appreciates color and composition, this view must be inspiring to her. We spend so much time together that I've learned to admire how different hues blend, and I'm already wondering how she'll recreate our current view with thread.

The sunrise paints the sky a bruised navy blue in the early dawn light, incrementally brightening to cobalt blue and finally settling on a magnificent azure. The sun's rays dance on a bubbly cloud crawling over the horizon, rendering it in shades of buttermilk, amber and gold, pastel and baby pink, and tipping it in snow-white.

The sea mirrors the symphony of colors, keeping me entirely fascinated, too enraptured to speak.

Yet I somehow find myself wondering about Everett. Is he also sitting on his balcony enjoying the view? Or are dhampirs more night owls? There's something about him that really piques my curiosity, the male occupying most of my thoughts since my first glance at his jade-green eyes.

A soft knock at the door breaks our bubble of tranquility.

"Come in," I croak, not bothering to take my gaze off the spectacular view.

"Beautiful."

I snap my head around at the sound of that voice. Expecting him to be staring at the sea, I'm caught off guard to see Everett's attention fixed on me.

It should be illegal to look as good as he does so early in the morning. He's dressed in all black, the epitome of elegance with his linen shirt tucked into his tailored wool silk pants. His dark hair flops artfully onto his forehead while a hint of stubble frames his jaw.

"Morning." It sounds more like a question than a greeting, but he doesn't look bothered by my lack of eloquence, rather amused.

"Incredible view, isn't it?" Again, he's staring directly at me and not even attempting to hide his flirting.

He looks so confident, leaning against the wall, hands in his pockets, and one leg crossed over the other at the ankle. The picture of arrogance. But what a delicious picture he makes.

I slept surprisingly well last night, so if he wants to play this game at the crack of dawn, I can play too.

"A downright feast for the eyes. Wish my other senses could also have some... fun." I rake my eyes up and down his body.

He stands up a bit straighter, eyes sparking. "What kind of fun do you have in mind?"

I lean back in my chair and pretend to think about it, taking my time to stare at him while I part my mouth and slowly run my tongue along my teeth.

"Oh, my goodness. Not to interrupt whatever is going on here, but I think it would be best if I excuse myself right now. Morning, Everett. Dede." Cece makes a run for the bathroom, the lock clicking into place once she's inside.

"I was just hinting at breakfast," I say innocently, forming my lips into a pout. Looking up at him, I feel my smile pulling my lips into something more mischievous and add, "My sense of taste could use some... satisfaction. Think you can satisfy that need?"

I feel like I'm playing with fire here, and it is so much fun watching all the different emotions flit across his face as he processes my words.

"Oh, sparkles. I can leave you very satisfied," he purrs. "Breakfast first, though."

He zooms over to me and holds out his right hand. I shrug off the throw blanket and place my left hand in his, nearly sighing at his touch, calmness blooming over the rest of my skin and settling in my chest. Too late, I notice the devilry spark in his eyes. He pulls me up—clearly showing off that extra strength of his—and I fly forward, losing my balance. In any other circumstance I might have thought I'd end up sprawled on the ground, but I also know this was by design, so I let go—and trust him to catch me.

He does.

I'm plastered to his body as he wraps his free arm around me, splaying his left hand across my lower back. My own free hand is pressed against his firm chest.

For a moment, neither of us moves. We just take each

other in, our breathing in sync.

Feeling overwhelmed by my visceral reaction to him, I push back a little. "Is there coffee with this breakfast?"

The corner of Everett's mouth tips up and he bands his arms a little tighter around me, then zooms us into the room and stops close to the door. I press my lips together to keep the squeal from escaping, not willing to give him a strong reaction.

He reluctantly lets me go, trailing his fingers along my waist as he steps back. "Anything you want, sparkles." He actually sounds sincere right then. "Head up to the dining room when you're ready. It's in the main building, on the other side of the great room we were in last night. I can hear most of the other women are already up and about, but maybe let them know there's food and coffee available."

"Sure, I'll go around and tell them to head up." I give him a small grin.

"By the way, you look wonderfully tantalizing in nothing but my clothes," he purrs, hungry gaze eating me up.

In a blink, he's gone, the door snicking shut quietly behind him.

My feet are rooted to the spot, and I stare at the closed door. Behind me, I hear Cece exit the bathroom.

"Dede, you're going to have to do something about all that chemistry. He's not my type, but I swear even I was about to combust back there." She fans her face dramatically and turns to the mirror to start finger combing her freshly washed hair.

"Right?! His banter is next level. Add that to his pretty green eyes, the thick brown hair, the strong jaw... Such an enticing package." I put the back of my hand to my forehead and fake a swoon. "Not to mention his body. He looks like he should be posing on the cover of *Vanity Fair*."

I'd for sure buy a copy. Or two.

"Do you think he has? What's his job? Do dhampirs have jobs?"

"He said something about a hotel last night, but I'm not sure what he does. Let me grab a quick shower too, and then we can gather up the girls for coffee and breakfast in the dining room." I pause, realization dawning painfully. "Cece. I'm not wearing any makeup. That's something I usually save for a third date. I look so different from last night without my winged eyes or my lips painted." I'm slowly freaking out.

"I can assure you, he more than appreciated your face this morning. He was definitely interested last night, but I think even more so this morning. I can only imagine the two of you dialed things up a notch after I excused myself. Am I correct?" Cece's chin dips and her brows raise.

She's not wrong.

"Um, yeah. There's just something about him. I'm drawn to him, fully aware of his presence. I can't quite explain it, but it feels... 'more.'"

"I get it," she murmurs, barely audible, turning back to the mirror.

"What? Have you had this before? Wait. You never got around to telling me where your tattoo is or who's your partner."

Have I been so self-absorbed that I didn't remember to ask her? She was asleep by the time I got to our room last night.

"No, nothing as intense as you're experiencing. We haven't made any physical contact yet, so I think that's helping. And you and Everett seem naturally attracted to each other, despite this tattoo thing. My partner, on the other hand, is most certainly not attracted to me. He's hardly aware of my existence." She's not making any eye contact, just vacantly staring at the floor as she runs her fingers through her hair.

I walk over to her and grab her hand. Squeezing it, I gently ask, "Cece, who?"

She finally lifts her gaze and meets my eyes. I take a moment to study her, and I see so much that she's been trying to hide. There's confusion, embarrassment, sadness, and... dare I say, longing?

Cece takes a deep breath in. With watery eyes and a wobbly smile, she breathes out, "Adelbert."

12

Everett

The ladies enter the dining room as a pack, chatting and sticking close together. Their eyes roam over all the males already gathered there, and they go quiet as their gazes linger on Edmond, who now has his wings out.

With the ring's power, he still looks human—except for the batlike wings protruding from his back. Despite his reluctance, we were able to convince him to stretch his wings before he needs to confine them again for the journey back to Paris.

All the males woke early to prepare a lavish breakfast in the hopes that the women would more easily accept the news we have to break to them on a full stomach.

Because of the different species present, we have a variety of dietary needs covered. We didn't have to ask them their preferences because there's something for everyone.

After spending most of the night in the library discussing options, we settled on something we know won't be met well. It was, however, the best we could do given the circumstances, the timeline, and the limited information available.

Trying to put my flirting on a simmer for the duration of breakfast, I walk over to Sadie and, in as much of a neutral tone as I can muster, ask, "How do you take your coffee, sparkles?"

"Black."

My head rears back. "Seriously?"

"Why? Think you know me well enough to predict how I'd take my coffee?" Sadie asks with hands on her hips.

"Not well enough... yet." I wink.

Dammit! *Less* flirting. I promised myself I'd wrestle it under control for the next hour.

"Okay, zooms. How did you think I'd take it?" she challenges me.

My brows shoot up. "Zooms?"

"What? Thought I'd forget to give you your own nickname? You never walk, always zooming in and out of rooms. If that's what you're going to do, then that's what I'm going to call you. Zooms." She says all this with her back ramrod straight, arms crossed over her chest, chin tilted defiantly.

It's hot.

"Well, sparkles. If I had to wager, I'd say you prefer a latte. Something sweet. Preferably caramel, but vanilla would also do. And on particularly indulgent days, you'd add a fuck ton of whipped cream on top. But what do I know?"

Her mouth hangs open. "How did you—"

"But since you prefer black, let me 'zoom' over there and get you a nice, strong, bitter black coffee."

"Wait." Sadie makes a grab for my arm, and I smirk down at her.

Raising my eyebrows expectantly, I watch her worry her lip between her teeth.

Finally, she sighs. Visibly deflating as she comes to a decision.

"Do you have caramel here?" she asks hesitantly with her eyes closed, nose scrunched up.

I can see it's taking a monumental effort from her to bite back whatever sarcastic remark is on the tip of her tongue. Coffee is apparently way more important than proving a point. Noted.

"We actually do. Jasper has a sweet tooth, and we stock a selection for him," I explain, thankful for our resident candy addict's requests.

Sadie's eyes pop open, hope restored as her whole being lights up. "And how do *you* take your coffee?" she asks.

I move to lean against the wall and cross my arms over my chest. "Guess."

"Black?"

A slow smile spreads across my lips. "Looks like you know me too."

And try as I might, I can't resist another wink. *Might have to see a healer about that.*

Everyone grabs plates of food and gathers around the long table that can comfortably seat eighteen. It's a beautiful solid slab of black walnut, custom made for the spacious dining room, a tasteful complement to its high ceilings.

Due to their sheer size, Harvey and Sawyer bring two additional chairs to seat themselves at opposing ends of the table so they can eat comfortably and someone doesn't get hit with an elbow in the face. Edmond, needing room for his wings, takes a low-backed chair around the center where he can stretch them out behind his companions.

Erik then directs Jamie and Jasper to seats away from each other, placing Rollo and Daehan as calming buffers next to them. I chuckle to myself at Erik's thoughtful supervision of those two. They're the biggest troublemakers, and whenever they're together, shit is bound to get wild or weird.

Predictably, the women stick to the opposite side of the table from the males. Though, there's an air of comradery as we enjoy our meals, low conversations striking up here and there as the sun slowly climbs higher in the sky.

The tranquility from outside has seeped into the dining room through the folding doors that have been pushed back. The gauzy curtains flanking our view of the Caribbean Sea dance gracefully in the light breeze. The birdsong is a harmonious addition to a picture-perfect morning on a tropical island.

Once everyone seems about done with their food, Sawyer patting his now-distended stomach in satisfaction, Bertie looks to me, and I give him a supportive grimace. It's time.

Bertie positions himself at the head of the table, and Harvey scoots out of the way to give him the limelight. "Good morning, ladies and monsters. I trust that you had a pleasant night's sleep."

Everyone gives him affirming but hesitant nods.

"After extensive research and much deliberation, I have concluded that the information needed pertaining to the marks is not available in this library, and I will therefore need to return to Alberad School for the Supernatural in Germany to scour its more comprehensive resources. The instant I find an answer to a means of dissolving the mark, I shall contact each of you. I hope to do this in an expedited manner so as to not inconvenience you or disrupt your lives any further than you have already experienced. My sincerest apologies for the events thus far."

I look across the table at Sadie and see the nerves I'm trying to hide reflected in her eyes. My heart is pounding furiously at what's to come next. I can't look away from her, but I'm carefully attuned to each word out of Bertie's mouth.

"Due to the distance limit that has come into effect with the marks, I have determined—for the best interest of each individual present—that you shall have to remain with your partner as you leave the island and accompany each other until this matter has been resolved."

"You just expect us to..."

"I'm not leaving with a stranger for..."

"This is unbelievable."

"Who do you think..."

The women all start talking at the same time, and a chair is pushed back noisily. Bertie raises his hand and silently exerts an imperceptible amount of his magic to bestow calm on everyone. I'm only aware of what his magic can do since I've known him for eighteen years, but he usually tries to hide his abilities. I know he respects autonomy too much to interfere with others' lives.

"If anyone present can provide a more feasible alternative, I would more than welcome hearing it." I can see the effort he's putting into keeping his face passive and open, nonthreatening.

Elves are haughty by nature and can look very intimidating. But Bertie is incredibly clever and knows how to read a situation and adapt accordingly, a skill that's oddly missing when it comes to his dating life.

I note the deep Vs between furrowed brows as the women concentrate. One woman is even biting her nails in contemplation. But no one comes forward with an idea.

"This is my business card. Please contact me at any time should you have any questions. I will ensure that I'm available. No matter the time zone differences, you are always welcome to contact me, day or night, phone calls, text messages, or emails." He goes around the table and personally hands each woman his business card, taking care not to accidentally brush against them.

Returning to his original position, he addresses the room again. "I have removed the wards blocking cellular services. You should be able to make arrangements freely now. I do, however, ask that you refrain from mentioning this island or alluding to its location." He pauses and waits for us all to nod before continuing.

"For now, I will ask you to speak to your partner. You can decide between yourselves where you will live for the foreseeable future. I cannot yet provide you with a timeline, but I'm leaving today and will start my research tonight. It will be in everyone's best interest to leave as early as convenient, for once I am not present on this estate, I cannot take responsibility for your safety."

Sadie's face is completely blanched. I look to the other women. They're all sporting similar expressions of disbelief and dread. The air is turning sour with a slight scent of fear emanating from that side of the table.

Bertie notices the discomfort and holds up a finger. "Ah, before I forget, the most important element to guarantee your safety. It is imperative that you know that all the males have volunteered to swear an oath of safekeeping to you. Each oath will be tailored to the individual and his species and will be between you, him, and the fates. If you would like a witness, I will be present, or however many other witnesses you desire. At this point, I will ask you to make your way to your partner so you can start discussing your plans."

With that, Bertie turns and beelines for Florence, checking his watch on his way. Knowing Bertie, I'm sure he's worked himself into knots over all this. He's not one to force anyone to do anything, but it's not like he can follow Florence to Kentucky. He *needs* to go to Germany. Which means, so does Florence.

I zip to Sadie's seat and lean against the dining table across from her. I aim for casual, but a note of concern still seeps into my voice. "You okay with everything Bertie just said?"

Sadie takes a deep breath before she answers on a slow exhale. "I'm okay. I think. My worry is more about Cece, though. She has to go to Germany."

"Bertie will take good care of her. You don't have to fret about that." My hands ache to comfort Sadie, but I keep them wrapped around the edge of the dining table, unsure if she would welcome my touch while processing all the new information.

Sadie toys with the hem of my T-shirt she's still wearing. Her brow pinches as she looks up at me with eyes the color of the ocean, unease swirling in their depths. "Would he, though? It looks like he's going to be wrapped up in research all the time. And I *know* my sister, she's not one to ask for any favors. I'm nervous about her being lonely and unhappy in a strange place."

Unable to resist any longer, I reach for her hand and trace her knuckles with my thumb. "He might not look attentive, but I can assure you, Bertie will try to make her feel comfortable."

Sadie folds her lips between her teeth and swallows hard. "Okay. I believe you. I'll just have to check in with her every day."

"I can also check in with Bertie from time to time. If you want?"

My offer seems to surprise her as she blinks a couple of times and stumbles out, "That's... Thanks."

I let go of her hand and lean back again. Shifting gears, I ask, "Do you have any pressing matters to take care of in Kentucky?"

"No, not for a while. It's summer break, so I can be flexible. And don't you dare make a joke about 'flexible.' I can already see your thoughts churning." She points an accusing finger at me, and at the same time, I see the mischief playing at the corners of her eyes and mouth. "Not that this has anything to do with you, but I *am* flexible."

My mouth does this odd thing where it's opening and closing like a fish out of water. My brain is scrambled. Visions of Sadie in all kinds of pretzely positions burst through my mind. Before I can get my wits in line to utter a retort, she speaks.

"You want me to go to Vegas with you, zooms?"

"I can't think of anything better."

"Vegas it is." Sadie tries to keep her face impassive and fight her excitement, but she fails spectacularly and lets a dazzling smile burst forth, toes tapping excitedly under her chair.

13

Sadie

After breakfast, we all return to our rooms to wash up and process what Adelbert said. The news was met with shock by some and denial by others, but I might have spotted a bit of excitement scattered among the women. It was definitely not just from me.

"I'm so happy for you, Dede. I know you've always wanted to go to Vegas. I bet you're happy you packed your fancy shoes. You'll fit right in over there." Cece's ever-present sunny side shines through her words, but looking into her eyes, I can see the nerves clouding her smile.

"Oh, Cece." I take her hands in mine. "Are you going to be okay? I think Germany is going to be beautiful. And didn't they say the school is in the Black Forest? Think about all the inspo you can get for your embroidery. You can make mad money with those pieces."

I try to encourage Cece to see the silver lining in moving to Germany for a while by focusing on the things that'll make her happy. Despite Everett's assurances that Bertie will be good to her, I can't help but think that Bertie will be holed up in the library, too focused on fixing this whole thing for everyone to pay Cece much attention.

Cece tries to hide her grimace as she sinks down on the bed. "I'd have to go buy thread and hoops. I didn't bring anything on this trip, just wanted to enjoy spending time with you. And I don't know if he'll be able to take time away from the library to indulge me much. There's a lot of pressure on him to resolve this as soon as possible. Who knows, maybe I'll see you back home in a week," she says, shrugging one shoulder.

The hope in her voice hurts like a paper cut to my heart.

She sits up suddenly, straightening her shoulders as she says brightly, "They have internet in Germany. I can just order supplies online if it becomes an extended thing." Cece's smile wavers, her shoulders slowly curling in again. "That's if... the wards allow it. But it'll be fine. Don't worry about me." She waves the comment away like it's no big deal, and listlessly starts folding the clothes she slept in last night.

I sit down next to my big sister and tuck one leg under me so I can face her more directly. "Cece..." I take the clothes from her hands and place them next to her. Grasping her hands in mine again, I wait for her to meet my eyes.

"You are an amazing, caring, intelligent woman. You give so much to everyone around you. You deserve to be the center of attention in someone's life. You deserve to be a priority. You deserve to have someone make an effort for you. You deserve to be seen. To be heard. To be loved. To be chosen."

Cece sucks in a fortifying breath and straightens her back. "You're right. I do deserve all that. And so do you." Suddenly serious, she says, "Dede, do you know how proud I am of you?"

"You are? For what?" I ask her, furrowing my brows as I rack my brain to find what prompted this shift in topic.

"I didn't say this yesterday, but before we move to opposite sides of the world, I want you to know how proud I am of you for going to school, getting your degree, and working so hard. I'm proud of you for what you've accomplished." Cece gives my hands a squeeze. "I hope I'm not overstepping, but sometimes it seems as if that spark you had when you started teaching has dimmed. Are you okay?"

My heart starts thumping powerfully in my chest, and I feel a flush spreading across my face and down my neck. I haven't said anything about my job to Cece. As it is, she worries so much about the people she cares about, so I didn't want to burden her. But she's as perceptive as ever.

Choosing to remain silent and letting her speak, I swallow hard around the lump in my throat and nod for her to continue.

Cece squeezes my hands once more and searches my face for something. Her voice is calm as she says, "If teaching isn't something that makes you happy anymore, if there's anything else you'd like to pursue, you've got my full support. I can always—"

Surging forward to give her a hug, I cut her words off before she can make a ridiculously generous offer. "I love you, you know that?"

I clear my throat, sit back, and quickly shift the focus of the conversation back to my sister. "I don't know what's happening with the males. I don't know how long this will take. But don't let Adelbert walk all over you. Don't allow him to make you an afterthought. Don't be afraid to stand up for yourself. I wish we were going with you so I can kick his ass if he's rude."

Narrowing her eyes playfully at me, she counters, "Don't make me come to Vegas and give Everett a piece of my mind if he doesn't treat you right, either."

I laugh her comment off, not worried about Everett. He's been great so far, and I'm actually kind of looking forward to this little getaway.

Cece places her hands on my shoulders and starts, "Sisters by blood."

I copy her gesture and complete our favorite expression. "Friends by choice."

Then we squeeze each other tight for the last time in who knows how long.

Letting go, she arranges her face into mock sternness, mischief twinkling in her eyes. "Do you need me to talk to Everett about protecting your virtue?"

I snort, and we both start giggling, which turns into semihysterical laughter and eventually tapers off into sniffles.

"I'm going to miss you." My voice wobbles as a tear tracks down my cheek.

Cece wipes my tear with her thumb, her chest rising with a deep breath. "I'll miss you too." Jutting her chin forward, she commands, "Now, let's move our cute butts and be on our way to our next adventures."

All the males and women have gathered in the great room, meeting in little huddles teeming with muted anticipation. The sun is now bright, and the warm air is charged with electric possibilities. Numerous goodbyes are said, hugs and numbers exchanged, and we separate into our pairings.

With each woman standing next to her partner, I can't help but think there's something serendipitous about it all. Like they suit the males next to them.

The males have elected to keep their rings on throughout our stay, and it's almost enough to forget that they're not human.

Except Edmond of course. His wings are still out but now tucked close to his body so as not to brush against Sylvia. He said something about waiting until the last moment before he'll glamour them again.

My eyes scan through all the couples. Natalie bounces on her toes—the sentiment reflected in the glint in Jasper's eyes as his gaze stays fixed on her. I can't quite remember where they're going, but they both look excited to get there. Unlike Sawyer and Louisa, both with arms folded over their chests as they lean against a far wall.

Iris steps forward. "Before we go, I'd just like to report on the captain and the yacht. Once Adelbert restored cellular services, I was able to contact the charter company. They have no record of the ship or the captain on their logs."

Adelbert runs a hand through his hair. With a shaky voice, he asks, "What was the name of the boat?"

"*Amarto.*"

A deafening silence descends on the room. All color drains from the males' faces. No one moves.

Iris quirks her head. "Uhhh... What am I missing?"

Adelbert clears his throat and, for the first time, stutters through his words. "That... that means... 'the fates' in Elvish."

The males are still as statues as we stare at them. My eyes bounce from one male to the next, feeling the weight of the pronouncement even if I don't understand it.

Everett's brows furrow into a deep V as he asks, "What could this even mean? Do you think the fates orchestrated all the events yesterday?"

My eyes track the goose bumps rising on his arms, the slight shudder working down his back.

Adelbert looks down at his feet and shakes his head slowly. He mutters more to himself than us, "This is much bigger than I thought. We need to leave right now so I can start my research." He looks up at Iris, his expression grim but determined. "Please stay in touch with the charter company and see if they can investigate this matter further. Report to me if you find anything useful." Turning back to the room, Adelbert steels his spine and purposefully makes eye contact with each of us. "For everyone else, I will arrange a group video conference as soon as any details have been uncovered. Thank you all for your patience and cooperation. Until we meet again."

And with a final nod to us, Bertie turns to leave, Cece trailing a step behind him—the two of them taking care not to accidentally touch each other. Before disappearing around the corner, Cece turns to give me a final wave, and I blow her a kiss.

The other couples, too, start trickling out of the room, on their way to various destinations around the world.

Everett raises his eyebrows at me. "That was intense."

"Yup." I drag the word out, contemplating how many more truth bombs I can handle. "It's like I want to ask what that was all about, but also not."

Everett gives me a lopsided smile. "I'll explain more later if you want. But first, I've got a surprise for you."

I perk up. "I'll *bite*. What is it?" I'm a sucker for surprises.

"Was that a vampire joke?"

I wink at him, and he just chuckles and takes my hand. "Follow me. It's in my room. And before you get ideas, don't worry, it's very PG."

Everett leads me to his bedroom. It's almost an exact replica of my room with its canopied bed in the center, only this one has sapphire-blue accents, where mine had mint green.

"I had my assistant go to your hotel and ask the staff to pack your belongings. I thought you might want to have your own things available in case you wanted to change into something more comfortable." He points to my bag on his bed.

"Oh, wow! That's very considerate. I thought we'd stop by there on the way back, but I guess this is more convenient."

I walk over to the bag to inspect it. All my clothes and shoes are there, not one item of Cece's. I thought they might have gotten some of our things mixed up.

As if reading my thoughts, Everett says, "I had your sister's bag sent to Bertie already."

When did he even have time to plan this? "Are you always thinking about everything, ten steps ahead?"

"Not particularly, but you're my guest and it's important to me that you feel comfortable," Everett says, his soft smile making him look even more beautiful.

"This guest is very grateful. Thank you. Sit tight, I'll be right back," I say as I take my bag to the bathroom.

14

Everett

Sadie rushes into my bedroom's en suite with her bag while I take a seat in the armchair by the window.

A couple of minutes later, the bathroom door clicks open. I look up and my breath catches in my lungs. I can't blink. I can't breathe.

I thought she looked great in the pink dress last night, even better in my clothing, but she's a showstopper right now.

I drop my eyes down to her sparkly pink toes and leisurely trail them up her body, perusing every detail. When I finally settle on her eyes, I can see she's not unaffected by my attention. A rosy red stains the apples of her cheeks, and her perky tits rise and fall on each shallow breath.

Those tits deserve a song dedicated to them.

They're a generous handful accentuated by her champagne-pink top. The top is tiny with puffy sleeves at the middle of her upper arms. It leaves her shoulders and cleavage on beautiful display and shows a sliver of skin across her stomach where it barely meets the skintight white jeans. Her sky-high stilettos, with their oversized pink bows, make her legs look like they go on for days, even if she only reaches up to my shoulders.

I want to devour her. I want to peel those jeans off slowly and trail open-mouthed kisses up from her ankles, alternating between legs, until I reach the apex of her thighs. I want to put my nose in the crook of her neck and inhale her, then nibble my way across her collarbones, down her chest until I get to her breasts. I want to find out what her nipples taste like. What sounds she makes when she's being pleasured. Will she scream? Whimper? Mewl?

I shift in my seat and try to discreetly adjust my cock. When did I get this hard from just looking at someone? This woman is magic. Sweet, sweet magic.

"Like what you see?" Apparently, I wasn't so discreet with my adjustment.

"You know I do," I say with complete honesty. "You look absolutely delectable."

I bite my lip to keep from saying more. My knuckles turn white from the sheer force I'm gripping my knees with, holding back. My hands aching to touch her. My tongue begging to taste her.

On my next inhale, I know I'm in big trouble. Sadie's sweet arousal is like a caress across my skin. Like a tangible embrace of all my senses.

"We should, um"—I clear my throat, trying to rid my voice of its sudden huskiness—"finish packing. My assistant, Pierce, is waiting outside."

"I'll give you a moment to think of puppies and rainbows while I finish up." She turns on her heel, flips her hair over her bare shoulder, and sashays across the room with extra sway in her hips.

I'm in big trouble with this beautiful enigma. Sadie is tempting this dhampir with every breath.

The thought reminds me that we got sidetracked during discussions and that I never got the chance to make an oath to her. This wrests me out of my lust haze faster than thinking of puppies or rainbows ever could.

"Sadie." My tone alerts her that I'm serious about what I want to say.

Her steps halt and she looks at me over her shoulder.

"Um, zooms? Are you okay?" Sadie's eyes jump around the room like she's searching for a missing threat.

"I'm okay. But I want to ensure that *you* are okay. Bertie talked about making an oath to our partners. I'm so sorry I forgot to make it earlier. You should've said something." I lightly scold her because I want her to feel safe with me, and somehow, it feels like she's not too worried about herself. Should I be double worried on her behalf, then?

"I'm really okay. But if it'll make you feel better, then oath away. I'm all ears. Or how do you want to do it?"

I walk over to her and hold my hands out, palms up in invitation. Sadie slowly puts her bag down on the bed then turns back to me. She places her small hands on top of mine, and I fold my fingers around her soft, dainty ones. Staring deep into her electric-blue eyes, I take a deep breath and start a personalized version of the oath my monster brothers and I settled on last night.

"Sadie. I vow to do everything in my power to keep you comfortable for the duration of your stay in Vegas. I will do my utmost to make this as much of an enjoyable experience for you until a resolution has been found. I swear by the fates that you are safe with me. I will not hurt a single hair on your head... unless you beg me to."

I wholeheartedly mean the entire oath, but couldn't help adding that final sentence. It just feels fitting for us to enjoy our time together and see if there's anything to this chemistry. But I will not touch her until she's practically begging me to. I understand I'm in a position of power and that she's moving in on my turf. But she's a very capable, educated woman who can make her own choices. If she wants to explore something, I'll be a very willing participant.

"Lovely oath. I appreciate all your careful words and can feel the weight of them. However... beg? You think I'm going to 'beg' you to touch me?" Her voice is ripe with incredulity.

"Well, yeah. I'm not in a position to make a move on you. I don't want to take advantage of you when you're in a vulnerable position." I try to explain it sincerely, but by the pursing of her lips, I can tell this is not going well for me.

"Vulnerable? So let me get this straight. You're going to take care of me and make sure I'm happy and comfortable in Vegas?"

"Yes."

"And you want me to enjoy myself while I'm there? For however long I'm there?"

"Again, yes."

"And even though we have incredible chemistry and you can't stop staring at my tits or my butt, you refuse to touch me unless I 'beg' for it?"

I swallow audibly and shift my weight to my other foot. "Yes."

"Got it." The smirk that climbs across her lips pushes her plump cheeks up, and her eyes dance with challenge. "We'll see who'll be begging first."

She slowly lets her tongue peek out between her teeth and delicately drags it along her lower lip. My gaze is ensnared on her luscious lips, my body fighting against the need to drag that bottom lip into my mouth and suck on it. To reach out and wrap her long blonde hair around my fist to angle her head just so, then I can delve my tongue into her mouth, tasting her. My hands—

Nope.

I take a large step backward and blink hard to clear the vivid image. My cock is a steel bar in my pants. Sadie stares at it, then back up at my face, and scoffs. She turns around and walks over to her bag, calmly rearranging the items inside and bending over exaggeratedly at every opportunity.

Neither of us says anything, but she's definitely made her point.

Round one: Sadie wins.

15

Sadie

After packing, Everett carries our bags down to a waiting car. I assumed it was a taxi, but then I notice how big and luxurious it is.

A bulky male stands by the open back door, his tawny skin glowing in the tropical weather, the sun reflecting off his bald head.

I don't know how I can tell, but now that I'm aware monsters live among us, he strikes me as not wholly human. He looks like he spends a lot of time lifting heavy stuff in the gym and probably eats a diet consisting mostly of protein.

With eyes crinkling in the corners, he offers us a genuine smile. "Mr. Ülavere, Miss Everly," he greets us in a warm, gravelly bass.

I raise a brow at Everett, mouthing, "Ülavere?"

He nods with a light cherry shade staining his cheeks.

Turning back to the large male still standing stoically next to the car, I smile at him in return. "Good morning, please call me Sadie," I say, offering my hand.

His gentle grip dwarfs my hand. He exudes kindness, and despite his towering size, I instantly feel safe and comfortable with him.

"Pleased to meet you, Sadie. I'm Pierce."

Everett places a hand on the small of my back and says, "Go ahead and get comfortable. I need to discuss something with Pierce real quick."

I scoot into the back while they exchange some words and then load our bags in the trunk before Everett joins me.

Pierce closes the door after him, enclosing us in the back with the privacy partition in place.

Once the car starts moving, I shift in my seat and turn fully to Everett. Whispering fiercely, I ask, "Are you like *rich* rich?"

"Define rich." He leans back oh so casually.

"That's something only rich people say." I point an accusing finger at him.

"You could say I come from a wealthy family. Most of the Vegas Strip is owned by vampires. I'm a bit of a black sheep since I'm a dhampir and not a 'pure' vampire." His shrug is apathetic, but I can taste the bitterness in his statement.

"Uh, what? Own? The Vegas Strip? Vampires?" My voice rises with every word, my incredulity growing with its volume. Then, in a whisper, I add, "Does Pierce know about all that? Is it safe to talk about that here?"

"Oh, Pierce knows almost everything about my life. He's a golem and has worked for me right from the start. Good male, very kind, very loyal."

I blink. Then blink some more.

"It's going to take me some time to process this. My brain kind of feels like it's melting. Any other necessary information you need to divulge before my brain shuts down completely?"

"A couple of things," Everett admits with a barely perceptible cringe. "Do you want them in quick succession or revealed piece by piece over the span of the journey to Vegas?"

Vegas.

It just hit me: I'm on my way to a new city with a supernatural being I met yesterday, who is apparently very rich and incredibly handsome and a wonderful flirt. And I don't know for how long.

"You better tell me in quick succession because I'm gonna start spinning out very soon."

"Okay. We're on our way to a small airport where we will board my plane. Flight will be about six hours. Once we're in the air, I'll most likely have a bunch of phone calls to make and messages to respond to since I've been out of reach while on the island. Please don't take my preoccupation personally, but I am expecting to have a couple of pressing matters I have to see to. Once we land, I'll drive us to my hotel, where I've arranged a suite for us to share. Don't worry, it has two bedrooms. Because of the distance limit, I thought it would be better for us to stay there instead of at my place. I'll also do all my work from the suite, so it'll be more convenient for you to move around and explore the area given our distance limit. Considering how many floors up we'll be, we're going to have to experiment to see how far our range is without hitting that invisible wall. Let's see, what else?"

Everett crosses his arms and worries his bottom lip with a long canine. "Pierce will see to it that your flight is canceled and make sure you are reimbursed. I tend to keep to a night schedule, seeing as vampires don't do daylight and most of my business is with them. But it's July in Vegas—you don't want to be out in the daytime much anyway.

"If there is a show you want to see, a restaurant you want to try, ask me, and I'll arrange it. If you need anything from me, I'll make myself available for you. Day or night. Anytime. I promise to try to make this adjustment as easy and comfortable for you as possible."

"Huh?" My mouth hangs open, my blinking unnaturally slow.

"Do you need me to repeat some of that?" Amusement plays at the corners of his mouth.

I shake my head. "No. Maybe. I don't know. Hotel? Like you work at a hotel?"

"My family owns a few, but Auvere Hotel is mine." He's not boasting when he says it, but his pride in his hotel is clear.

"The Auvere? That's... yours?" I ask incredulously, looking at the male in front of me through a different lens.

He's not once flaunted his wealth or status, and I find myself appreciating this side of his character.

"Yup, do you know it?" Surprise widens his eyes.

"It's on my mood board." I did not mean to say that out loud.

"Is it, now?" The serpentine smile Everett gives me is nearly lethal. "What was the theme of this board?"

"I'm not telling you. You'd have to 'beg' me." My grin is smug.

"You want me to beg you, sparkles?" Everett's words are a dangerous purr, making the tiny hairs on my nape stand on end.

"How bad do you want to know?" Crossing my arms, I try to feign nonchalance.

"I'd rather beg for something else." His eyes caress down my body and back up again.

"Would you now? Care to expand on that?" I try to call his bluff.

"I totally would, but the car has stopped and Pierce is very patiently waiting to open my door."

And with that, I'm zapped back to reality, the bubble of seduction officially popped.

I look out the window. We've arrived at an airfield. He wasn't shitting me.

How did I get so distracted to not notice that the car had stopped?

I lift my chin and tuck my hair behind my ear, the picture of cool indifference. If only this silly blush would stop heating my cheeks, then it might be a little more convincing. "What are you waiting for? Let's go, zooms."

Everett shoots me a bemused smile and subtly shakes his

head. "Your wish is my command, sparkles. Wait right there."

He gets out of the car and indicates to Pierce that he'll get my door. With one hand on my open door, Everett bows slightly at the waist and holds out his other hand expectantly. When I place my hand in his, he curls his fingers around mine and pulls me up, leading me to the airplane. *His* airplane.

As we climb the stairs, the flight attendant greets him by name while Pierce loads our luggage.

Everett gestures for me to choose a seat first, then takes the seat next to mine on the opposite side of the aisle, the distance between us a reprieve.

The attendant is friendly and professional, supplying us with refreshments the moment we're settled.

Then the pilot comes out of the cockpit, greeting Everett like an old friend, and explains the flight plan to us.

My head is still spinning with everything Everett just unloaded on me in the car. I don't think I can handle anything more, never mind carrying on a conversation, so I nod along blankly to whatever is said.

I turn to the window once the pilot heads back to the cockpit and stare blankly out at the verdant mountains in the distance. I don't comprehend that the airplane has taken off until the sight below me has changed to lush islands encircled by crystal-clear cyan-blue waters, dark teal ocean spreading out beyond.

The attendant moves inconspicuously around the plane, keeping Everett and myself fed and hydrated as I keep my face plastered to the window and he works with single-minded focus on his laptop, his phone nearly glued to his ear for the duration of the flight.

I don't try to listen in, nor do I mind the lack of opportunities to talk to him. My brain has reached its capacity for the day, and I need the time to think and process.

I wonder how Cece is doing and if she'll be able to enjoy her time in Germany. I'll text her once I'm settled. But right now,

I can't think beyond my own circumstances, wondering what the next couple of days—or however long it's going to take Adelbert—will look like for me.

Eventually, I get my thoughts under control and have an impressive desire to disassociate before we land in my new reality. I turn my personal screen on and flick through the library of reality TV shows they have.

Like the fates have designed it, I find the latest season of a dating show on a tropical island that I like to watch. I get engrossed in the show and blissfully tune the rest of the world out until the airplane's wheels kiss the tarmac in Vegas.

In what feels like no time at all, we're disembarking in the middle of the scorching desert.

My home for the foreseeable future.

Sadie: Just landed in Vegas

Sadie: Everett is rich. Like, owns-a-hotel rich

Sadie: Message me when you get to Adelbert's place. I want DETAILS!

Everett

Our flight arrives around sunset, the summer heat still unbearable. We hurry to my car to escape the dry desert temperatures and blast the AC. A slight sheen of sweat covers my skin from the short time outside, whereas Sadie looks cool and composed, like she's ready to walk a runway.

Once our bodies have cooled enough and I can lower the blast of the AC, I turn to Sadie. "Are you ready to see Vegas?"

"Yeah." She's not one-hundred-percent convincing as she nods, but it's enough to know she's not spinning out anymore.

I arranged for my car to be waiting for us, wanting to drive her to the hotel myself while Pierce takes our luggage directly there. On the plane, I was so preoccupied with work and making arrangements for our stuff to be moved to the suite before we arrived that I wanted to take the time in the car to check in with her.

"I'm going to drive you the long way in. I want you to get the maximum first impression of Vegas." *And I want to see your face as you take it all in for the first time.*

"That's... considerate." A line forms between her brows as she cocks her head at me, seemingly trying to puzzle out my thoughtfulness.

I gave Sadie space on the plane because I thought she

needed time to process all the information I dumped on her. I want her to feel comfortable with me, and having a moment alone before she's thrust into my world might be good for us both.

"Anything for you, sparkles." I try to lighten the mood by adding a wink, which has served me well so far with her.

"Anything? Don't tempt me," Sadie warns with an imperiously arched brow.

There she is. Confident Sadie is back. What a queen.

"Just you wait." I hit her with the sauciest smirk I can muster and waggle my eyebrows.

We're silent for most of the drive, the sky darkening as we make our way toward the hotel. I take back roads through more residential areas, building the suspense on the way to the main attractions. In the distance, the bright lights of the Vegas Strip lure us with every mile we pass.

I drink Sadie in as she takes in the view. Watching her face light up as we make our way through the streets of Vegas is unexpectedly gratifying.

Wanting, no, needing to know more about her, I ask, "What are you most excited to see or do in Vegas?"

She doesn't look at me, keeping her eyes fixed on the sights out the window, as she mumbles, "It's embarrassing to admit."

"I didn't think you'd be embarrassed by much. Come on, it's a safe space. Tell me," I coax, reaching over to give her hand a squeeze.

"It's not so much about the shows or the clubs or the casinos that I want to see. I actually just like the vibes of Vegas and the excuse to dress up. If you haven't noticed, I have a love for glittery things, and I tend to stand out like a bedazzled thumb back home. Vegas seems like it will indulge my fashion choices," Sadie admits, her finger drawing patterns on the back of my right hand where I'm still holding her left.

I smile to myself at how easy things feel between us. Physical touch and truthful admissions seem to come naturally, and I'm not about to lose a shot with the most interesting woman I've ever met.

"I like your sparkly style. It's a good contrast to my everyday, boring black. And if you want an extra excuse to dress up even fancier, I'll be sure to schedule events for us to attend. Vegas is going to make you feel right at home."

"No need for special events, zooms. But tell me, what's with the black outfits anyway?" Sadie asks, gesturing to my black-on-black clothing choice.

My shoulders lift on a shrug. "It's easier to fade into the background and keep an eye on things at work. And takes less mental space when I have to pick something to wear."

"Pft, please. Like you could ever fade into the background with a face like that," she says with a roll of her eyes, then immediately slaps a hand over her mouth.

"You saying you like my face, sparkles?" I tease her.

"You know what you look like." She shifts in her seat and moves her gaze to the window again. "Now, keep your eyes on the road while I study the view."

I decide not to rile her further and keep silent as I watch her eyes bounce from building to building, seemingly trying to catch every detail and commit it to memory. She's mesmerizing to watch, but I try to stay focused on the road.

All too soon, we're pulling up to the Auvere's entrance.

"Stay right there," I tell Sadie as she unbuckles her belt.

I walk around the car and throw greetings back to the guys on duty, deterring them from getting Sadie's door for her. I want to do that.

I open the door and give her my hand. She doesn't even hesitate to place hers in mine. The feeling of her placing her trust in me so easily has my stomach doing some weird somersaults and my heart beating in a staccato rhythm at what this could mean for the future.

Trying to distract myself from the feelings she's inciting

in me, I pull her up and forward until she's flush with my body. Allowing my free hand to rest on her waist, I hold her in place as I put my mouth right next to her ear.

"Welcome to your new home, sparkles."

I can physically feel a tremble rolling down from her shoulders to her feet.

Before she can come up with a snarky retort, I take a step back. Keeping a firm grip on her hand, I lead her through the opulent lobby.

The lobby's design is modern monochrome, with golden accents and lush greenery. Comfortable white couches are interspersed with classic, high-backed armchairs in black and gold. Low tables decorated with fresh blooms complement the indoor plants placed strategically around the high-ceilinged room. A massive chandelier, descending in a spiral of ginkgo leaves made from bone china, is the focal point of the lobby, with many people stopping to take pictures in front of it.

Sadie's feet drag as she tries to slow me down. Her eyes can't stop roaming, but I can see how she's fighting to look unaffected and keep her poise. I'm enjoying seeing her warring with herself like this.

Thoroughly distracted, I don't notice Alexandra until she steps directly into our path. The shit-eating grin she's sporting has my guts tightening.

"Welcome back, Everett," she drawls, her voice raking down my spine with its creepy claws.

"Alexandra." My tone is flat, making it clear I'm not in the mood for her crap.

Her eyes land on Sadie. With her lip curling back, Alexandra says, "Is this your new plaything?"

Before I can formulate a response, Sadie speaks up.

"This plaything has a name, I'm Sadie." She gives Alexandra a saccharine smile that's fooling no one.

Sadie impresses me with how quickly she's playing the

game, probably smelling Alexandra for the rat she is.

"A woman who knows her place. Delighted." Alexandra lets her eyes roam down Sadie's body, irking me to a whole new level.

"You'll watch yourself when speaking to her. Better yet, don't speak to her at all. What the fuck are you doing here anyway?" My tone is harsh. I'm confused as to why she's even in my hotel.

"Just passing through," she says innocently.

Sadie watches this exchange quietly, making me want to remove her from this woman's presence before Alexandra can inflict verbal damage.

"I think you better leave right now, or I'll have you escorted out," I say sternly, making a show of looking for my security.

Alexandra takes a step toward the exit. "See you around, Everett. Sadie."

Clasping Sadie's hand tighter in my now-sweaty palm, I start pulling her toward the private elevator.

"You know, your father would want to know you have someone staying with you. Indefinitely." Alexandra's parting words hit me like a backhand to the face and stop me dead in my tracks.

How could she possibly know about Sadie's arrival today, let alone her existence? Unless her little spies have been whispering things to her. I've tried to keep Sadie's stay not exactly a secret, but there are only a certain number of people who know I'm moving into a suite with a guest for an undetermined period of time.

I turn around slowly and narrow my eyes at her. "Don't threaten me in my own hotel. I don't know or care how you found out about her, but you'll keep your mouth shut. Sadie has nothing to do with my father," I grit out, my jaw aching with how hard I'm clenching it.

"Now who's the one doing the threatening? Have a good night, you two." She does a little finger wave before she saunters away, looking entirely unperturbed.

My shoulders are tense as we resume walking, and I loosen

my death grip on Sadie's hand but don't let go. I don't want my father to know about her. I have a fierce need to protect Sadie, more than my oath I swore to her requires.

I've felt this way since the first moment I saw her in the forest. This stunning woman with the heart-shaped face and beguiling blue eyes. My connection to her is growing stronger with every moment we spend together.

We enter the elevator in silence, Sadie most likely reading my tense mood. I don't even realize I started doing it, but I become aware that my thumb is tracing back and forth on Sadie's hand.

"Do I need to know who that was?" she asks.

"That was Alexandra," I sigh. "She works for my father, who is worse than she is. She might think herself his second-in-command, but she's human. He'll never truly value her. It's important to know she's schemy, always trying to prove herself to my father. So if, by chance, you bump into her again, don't engage with her. She'll try to get under your skin."

"Got it. Alexandra: bad human. Your father: bad vampire. Stay clear of both." Sadie gives me a resolute nod.

"Exactly. I'd *never* want you to meet my father," I confirm vehemently.

Her head jerks back like I've struck her, hurt clear in her eyes.

I'm about to explain how evil my father is and that I'm just trying to shield her from him when our elevator dings.

"I doubt I'll be around long enough to meet him anyway, so don't stress about it." She removes her hand from mine and pats me on the chest as she exits onto our floor.

I'm not quite sure what exactly I said that would elicit that response, but I resolve to ask her later and follow her out of the elevator.

"I'm sorry if I said the wrong thing back there."

"Seriously, no worries. Which one is our room?" she asks a little bit too brightly.

Taking her cue, I shift gears, hoping to get her back to the excited state she was in pre-Alexandra.

I walk slightly ahead of Sadie as I lead her down the hallway to the last room on the floor, her heels quiet on the plush gray carpet. "I know you were looking forward to Vegas and the lights, so when I had to pick a suite, this was the only one that would do."

"Why this one?" Sadie asks, craning her head to look for any clues.

"It's our best suite. Only this one's view could rival your shine."

"You saying I'm going to have competition?" Sadie asks with challenge clear in her eyes, one hand on her cocked hip.

"I'm saying it can try, but I'd much rather stare at you," I reply, biting my lip as I give her a lascivious once-over.

Her delighted expression causes something in my chest to flutter, making my smirk slip into a lopsided smile.

Key card in hand, I ask, "Ready for your new home, sparkles?"

She tilts her chin up. "I was born ready."

I place the card on the lock and push the door open once it beeps. Discreetly wiping my weirdly clammy palm on the front of my pants, I usher Sadie in with a hand on the small of her back.

I have a feeling things are about to get even more interesting.

Sadie

I walk into the luxurious living room, hardly taking in its blue-and-gold aesthetic, and immediately run over to the floor-to-ceiling windows, pressing my hands up against the glass. The neon lights, like bright beacons in the dark, tempt me closer like a moth to a flame.

The view is better than the photos I've seen online, my eyes jumping from one building to the next, trying to take in their details. For a second, I allow myself to forget about all the events that led up to this moment and just breathe. The only thing that would make it better would be if Everett came up behind me and pressed my whole body against the window with his, let his hands—

Nope. Not going there. No way am I begging him, despite what he said.

Yet, I can actually feel myself getting turned on by the image of us in front of this window, my pussy getting slick as I allow the picture to linger.

Stop thinking with your pussy, Sadie.

"Sparkles. Do you like our room that much?" Everett's voice is like a sweet caress from the other side of the room, causing my nipples to pebble.

"What do you mean?" How could he possibly know what's

going on in my head?

"My sweet sparkles, remember I said I have heightened senses? I can *smell* how wet you're getting."

Oh, fuck. I'm screwed. And not like how I want to be screwed.

I can feel the flush across my cheeks, burning my ears, making me too embarrassed to turn around in case I look like a flaming tomato.

I make eye contact with his reflection in the window. He's leaning against the doorframe, hands in his pockets, gaze riveted on me.

"I clearly have a love for shiny things, and this kind of exceeds expectations right now. You chose well and I'm just appreciating it," I admit, all nonchalant.

"I'm really enjoying the view too," Everett says, his voice like liquid seduction.

"You mean my butt? Or are you too shy to say that directly?" I taunt the monster boldly.

"Shy? No. But I am trying to be respectful." This man is all shades from sex to respect.

I shake my head in disbelief and counter with a casualness that belies the state of my panties. "Maybe I don't want you to be respectful."

"What do you need, sparkles? Tell me and I'll give it to you." Everett's baritone is now a whole octave lower, rough with lust.

"I don't think you can if you're being 'respectful.'" I add in quotes. "Sometimes a woman needs to be a little disrespected."

On my next blink, Everett is behind me. Close, but not quite touching. He reaches forward and moves my hair over my right shoulder, careful not to touch my skin. Then he bends down and skims his nose down the left side of my neck where it meets my shoulder.

Goose bumps erupt along my skin as I tilt my head to the right to grant him more access. He takes a deep breath in, then releases it on a sensual groan. My core clenches around nothing as the sound washes over me.

Everett reaches both arms around me to place his hands on the glass, right next to my own, caging me in but still not touching.

Keeping his nose in the crook of my neck, he lets his lips brush against the tender skin as he asks in a low voice, "What does being disrespected look like to you? Is it me touching you whenever and however I want? Is it playing with you until you're dripping and begging me to satisfy that ache? Is it a gentle hand around your throat right when you're about to climax? Is it me taking you right here, bending you over until you scream while you enjoy the view? Tell me what you need, sweetheart."

My breaths have become shallow pants. A tremor of arousal runs down my spine, pooling in my panties.

And now I know he can smell it.

In a breathy voice that doesn't sound like mine at all, I ask, "What if I say yes to all of the above?"

"Then just ask me, and I'll do everything I said... and more." The promise is plain in the growl of his voice.

"Just ask?" I pant.

Everett's response is smug as he takes a step back. "Ask? I meant beg."

The loss of his body makes me feel cold, yanking me out of the fantasy. I turn around and scowl, ready to lay into him. Then I see the evidence of his arousal tenting his pants.

Despite the arrogant mask on his face, it can't hide how affected he is by me too.

Donning a cocky expression, mirroring Everett's, I put a hand on my waist. I move my assessing gaze over his body, lingering on the telltale sign of his attraction to me.

With all my confidence in my own abilities, I say, "I told you I won't be the one begging. But you've just upped the stakes. Care to wager who will fold first?"

"So you agree that we are inevitable?" Everett counters.

"There's definitely chemistry. I wouldn't mind taking you

for a test drive. But I'm not a weak woman who can be dickmatized so easily. I don't *need* you, but I can admit that I'm curious to see if you can... satisfy me." I know phrasing it like this is playing with fire, though I can't help but think the burn would be oh so sweet.

Everett bites his fist. "Fuck, you're hot when you speak to me like that. Your confidence is hot. Everything about you is hot. This is going to be hard, but I'll take your wager."

"Okay, you fold and I get to order you around for a day. You'll have to do everything and anything I request. You in?"

Everett takes a moment to think it over. "Same if you fold?"

"I'm not going to fold," I say, laughing at the mere thought that I'd be the first to give in. I have a couple of tricks that will have him salivating before the end of the week.

"But if you do... do I get to order you around too?" Everett asks hopefully.

The gears turn in his head, and his eyes spark with the possibilities of what he'll request from me. Biting his long canine into his bottom lip, he takes the plush flesh between his teeth.

Trying not to seem affected by how sexy that move is, I shrug and give him a sweet smile. "Seems like a waste to say yes, but sure. If it'll make you feel better, then yeah, you can order me around too."

Everett surprises me when he asks, "Any ground rules?"

I didn't expect that. I thought it would only be a game to him. Asking for boundaries is respectful, so I consider my limits and answer, "Nothing mean. Teasing is okay, as long as it's between us."

"Done." He nods. "Let's shake on it."

We move to each other and thrust our hands forward. His rough hand engulfs mine.

Twirling a strand of hair around my finger on my free hand, I say sweetly, "I'm looking forward to seeing you sweat. Let me know when you're ready to cry mercy."

With all the confidence my wet panties can muster, I strut

over to the bedroom where my bag has been placed, feeling his eyes on my butt the entire way.

His sigh is loud when I close the door.

Cece: Arrived safely. His house is in the heart of the forest.

Cece: Everett owns a hotel? You're loving it, right? Send photos!

Sadie: Ceceeeeee, the hotel is beautiful. The view is EVERYTHING.

Sadie: This is the view from my room.

Sadie: *photo*

Cece: It's just like the pictures on your mood board. I'm so happy for you!

Cece: Getting settled into my room now.

Cece: The bed is heavenly. Look, I can make my own mood board with it.

Cece: *photo*

18

Everett

Despite the sexual tension last night and how close I came to ravishing her up against the window, I was good and went to my bedroom.

Trying to take advantage of being awake at the same time as my staff, I worked for a couple of hours before falling into a fitful sleep, thoughts of Sadie occupying my mind even then.

The temptation to rub one out to thoughts of her was strong, but it feels like a challenge to myself to not give in. If I climax, I want to do so while touching her amazing body and looking into her beautiful blue eyes. It would just be that much sweeter.

I thankfully don't have to worry about her going hungry since I requested that the suite be fully stocked. Not only loading the fridge in the kitchen with food, but also ensuring each bedroom's fridge was filled with healthy and not-so-healthy treats. I didn't want Sadie to have to ask for anything, but rather have it readily available. Now I can pat myself on the back for my forethought.

By the time I emerge from my room, it's late morning and Sadie is already awake. Not just awake, but she's in our suite's pool on the balcony.

In a bikini.

A very tiny metallic-looking bikini that only covers the

bare minimum.

She looks like sheer perfection, sitting on the step, leaning back on her elbows with her bottom half in the water. Sunglasses shielding her eyes from the harsh sun.

The glass balustrade in front of her grants an unobstructed view of the Strip, the crisp blue of the cloudless desert sky dwarfing the buildings stretching up like colossal metal thumbs beneath.

Sadie resembles an avenging angel looking down on her domain, plotting her conquest.

I could stare at her all day and not get tired of it. She could ask me to do her bidding, and I'd be all too happy to jump. I have this innate desire to make her happy.

With that thought in mind, I trudge to the suite's kitchen to make some coffee. Desperately in need of caffeine to distract me from the stunning image of her, I turn the machine on.

The noise has her looking over her shoulder at me, noticing me for the first time.

Shifting her sunglasses on top of her head, Sadie squints at me and calls through the open balcony door, "Any chance you can make me an iced caramel latte?"

"Sure," I say hoarsely and clear my throat. Then I add, "I already told the staff how you like to take your coffee, so all the ingredients should be here."

"You're a lifesaver, thank you." She beams.

I go about making our coffees but look up when, out of the corner of my eye, I notice movement. I'm so floored by the sight of her bare ass in the air that I drop the cup I'm holding, only for my reflexes to kick in at the last moment, grabbing it before it smashes to the ground.

"That's not playing very fair." My throat bobs with a hard swallow, and I resume making the coffee, trying to appear less rattled than I feel.

I wasn't sure Sadie heard me until I see the smirk on her face as she towels off the rest of her body. She definitely knows what she's doing.

"What's wrong, zooms? Don't like my bikini?" She asks playfully as she flicks the string of her top and drops her towel onto a nearby chair.

"It's fine," I say a bit gruffly.

"Just fine?" Sadie saunters into the kitchen and looks up at me, fluttering her eyelashes.

I know she's baiting me, but the image of her bending down to dry her legs will be imprinted on my brain for the rest of time.

"Maybe, um, don't turn around, or gods forbid, bend down in front of me again? Please?"

Sadie gives me an innocent look, her lips all pouty but with mischievous intent very clearly dancing in her eyes. "You mean like this?"

She turns around and languidly bends at the waist, brushing her fingers along her legs all the way down to her toes, flips her hair to one side, and peeks at me over her shoulder. Then, she wiggles her peachy butt at me.

My heart just about stops. I press a fist to my mouth to keep my words from spilling out.

That tiny thong hides nothing. I can see the outline of her pussy lips between her legs, lewdly begging me to touch, to stroke.

A groan rumbles out of my chest with a muffled "Sweetheart."

Batting her eyelashes at me, Sadie asks, "Are you ready to beg?"

That jerks me right out of it and I return my attention to her coffee.

"Nice game. I see what you're doing."

Sadie rolls her back as she slowly straightens and pads over to the other side of the kitchen. Leaning against the counter, she pushes those glorious tits out. "What am I doing, zooms?"

I don't trust that coy tone one bit.

"You're playing dirty. You want me to break first." I put down the cups and stalk over to her, stopping so close she has to tilt her head back to look at me.

"You've got so much to tempt me with. There's no way I can compete with the effect you have on me with this stunning body," I admit, my voice remarkably raspy.

Reaching out my right hand unhurriedly so Sadie can stop me at any time, I let my fingers brush along her collarbone. Wanting to confirm that she's okay with my touch, I shift my gaze from my fingers, where they're dancing across her skin, to her face. To the rosy color of her cheeks and her parted mouth. Sadie's almost as affected by my touch as I'm affected by touching her.

I move my hand down at a leisurely pace. I want her to be able to stop me at any moment if there's a chance I'm crossing a boundary she's not happy with. But the goose bumps in the wake of my touch and her rapidly increasing breaths let me know I've got the green light to continue.

I skim the backs of my fingers between the valley of her breasts to under the curve of her right breast. Her breath hitches, and it's like a physical touch that tugs on my cock.

I continue my patient exploration of her body, tracing the dip of her waist to the curve of her hips. When I reach the flimsy string of her bikini, I follow its line across her body, slowing my progress when I'm directly over her pussy. Not allowing myself to linger too long, I continue tracing the string to the other side. I shift my hand so the backs of my fingers drag over her left hip and continue their journey up, skimming across her ribs, under her left breast, up to her sternum.

When I reach Sadie's throat, I splay my hand lightly around her neck. Her breaths turn to pants, and my own breathing is labored. Our rapidly beating heartbeats synchronize in their rhythm. The scent of her arousal wraps around me, spurring me on.

I slowly trace her lips with my thumb, smearing her red lipstick on her bottom lip first, then her top lip as I circle her mouth.

When my thumb is back on her bottom lip, I push down slightly, and she opens her mouth a fraction wider.

The moment is electric. I feel like we're suspended in the air, supercharged in a cloud about to erupt in an electric storm. Like lightning waiting on the fringes to strike down at a moment's notice.

Sadie's tongue darts out to taste my finger. When I drag my gaze from her lips, I can see the want in her eyes. She nips at my thumb, and I push it deeper into her mouth, past the first knuckle. Closing her lips around it, she sucks, and I'm done for. My breathing turns ragged, and a hungry groan falls past my lips, my cock straining toward her.

I want to kiss this gorgeous woman. I want to consume her. Worship her. I want to bring her to such pleasurable heights that the mere thought of me makes her wet.

I ease my thumb from Sadie's mouth, and she chases it with another nip. Her nipples are so hard they're almost jutting through the flimsy material.

Sadie moves away from me and reaches for her coffee. She composes herself as she takes a sip, then with a self-satisfied smile in place, she does a little shoulder shimmy and singsongs, "You think I'm sexy."

"I thought we established that fact," I say flatly, adjusting my very obvious hard-on.

"You're not so bad yourself."

"Oh yeah? What do you like about me?"

Sadie looks my body up and down, tilts her head this way and that, and makes a motion for me to turn around. I do a slow spin for her and wait for her answer with bated breath.

"You're nice enough to look at," she says, all blasé.

I smirk back at her. "Liar. Your delicious scent has been spelling out exactly how attracted you are to me. When you did your little assessment of my body, it totally spiked, kind of like an unspoken confession. Besides that, you could've tried to convince me with your cool act, but the way your heart is galloping is kind of a dead giveaway."

"You can hear my heart?" Sadie asks, eyes as big as saucers.

"I can hear lots of little sounds, better keep that in mind for the rest of your stay."

"Pft. I was just joking." She rolls her eyes and waves a dismissive hand, clearly uncomfortable with being called out. "Not to change the topic or anything, but is there a plan for today?"

I take a sip of my lukewarm coffee and grimace. "I was thinking maybe we can head down around sunset and I can show you around the hotel. Last night went fast and might have been overwhelming on top of everything that's happened over the last two days. So, if you're up for it, let's maybe meet around eight?"

"Sounds good. Think I can go like this?" Sadie gestures to the scraps of material covering only her best bits.

I shake my head. "Sparkles. Please don't let me die at twenty-eight. You'd start a riot if you went downstairs looking this good, and then I'd have to fight each male off. I'd totally try, but success is not guaranteed when going up against certain species." I try to think about who we have scheduled to visit and if I could possibly fight them.

"Just kidding. I'll pick something that covers a bit more. But it's still going to be very much my style." Sadie adds the last sentence like she thinks I'm not going to approve.

"Wouldn't want you to be anything but yourself," I say sincerely.

The look she gives me is half surprised and half touched, as if the men in her past haven't truly appreciated her for exactly who she is. I'll be sure to regularly remind her how perfect she is.

19

Sadie

Everett is great. He's a masterful flirt and hits me with all the banter. He's freakishly good-looking, like can't-stop-staring, want-to-lick-him-from-head-to-toe gorgeous. But more than that, he's kind. He's so considerate and predicts my needs even before I know what I want to request. It's unreal. He's unreal.

If I'm not careful, I'm going to start catching feelings, and I don't think that's a good idea. I'm only here for a short while before I return to my very normal, nonglamorous life in small-town Kentucky, possibly teaching fourth graders again.

I'm going to focus on fun, flirt up a storm, and enjoy the attention while it lasts. Going to keep this heart safe.

I spent all afternoon going through my clothes, which were already hanging in my closet. Apparently, Pierce had raced ahead with our luggage while we took the scenic route. The magical faeries—not real faeries, just Everett's staff—unpacked everything for me before we arrived.

Opting for a gold sequined miniskirt and a backless black top, I look at my limited shoe options. Thank fuck I brought my dependable and versatile black strappy stilettos with the three-inch heel.

I might have to go shopping soon. My current clothing

choices are more suited for a tropical holiday, not the level of glitz and glam that Vegas requires. My usual preferences do have more sequins and shine than the average wardrobe, but if I'm going to be here, I want to go all out and live my best sparkly life.

I don't think I can afford to buy a new wardrobe, but maybe I could do a Vegas capsule collection. Or maybe they have rental shops for women like me, here for a short-term visit and in need of glitter-fying themselves. It would be awfully convenient.

Once I'm completely satisfied with my makeup, my curtain bangs are curled just the way I like, and my outfit has passed the three-sixty assessment in front of the mirror, I leave the room in search of Everett.

What I see, though, freezes my feet to the ground. My mouth hangs open, and saliva pools in my mouth.

Everett in a towel.

Only a towel.

Wet from the shower.

I'm committing this sight to memory. Excellent spank-bank material.

He sees me and swaggers his way over. Pausing awfully close, he places his hand under my chin and tilts my head up. With his thumb, he brushes the corner of my lips and whispers, "You had a little drool there."

Smug as hell, he turns around and swaggers back to his room, but not before he undoes his towel and lets it fall to the ground.

His ass is what inspires sculptors to create masterpieces. I'm not even ashamed of my ogling.

"See something you like, sparkles?" Everett looks over his shoulder, eyebrows raised, confident with his body—the picture of male perfection.

"Very much so. And you obviously know it." He was honest earlier, so this time it's my turn.

"I do." And with that, he moves to the opposite side, giving me a profile shot of what he's packing.

I'm intrigued. That thing is a weapon, and he's only sporting a semi.

Nevertheless, it's a weapon that I would like to rearrange my guts.

Trying to seem cool, like I see dicks that size on the regular, I throw out, "Better pack that anaconda away, don't want to scare the grannies at the slots."

His low laugh follows me on my way to the balcony, where I stop to take in the lights once again. I don't think it's possible for me to grow tired of this sight. Ever.
Such a pity that this little fantasy of playing house will come to an end pretty soon.

Sadie: CECE!

Sadie: I'm dead. Deceased.

Sadie: Everett. After shower. Naked. Hot. My eyes. Feast.

Sadie: *fire emoji* *melting emoji* *skull emoji*

Sadie: I know you're probably still sleeping. Ugh, time zones.

Sadie: Message me when you wake up. I need to verbally process what my eyes just saw.

Everett

It's so much fun teasing Sadie. The little competition we have going just keeps getting spicier and spicier. It's a ticking time bomb until one of us breaks.

She showed me earlier what she's working with when she pranced around the suite in those tiny scraps of material that she called a bikini. It was only fair that I return the favor by showing her what she could be playing with.

"Have I told you how exquisite you look tonight?"

Sadie's beautiful in her sparkly skirt and black top. But when she turned around, her bare back on display, I nearly came in my pants. She must know what she's doing to me. I can feel my control slipping with every minute I'm close to her.

"Not yet. But even if you had, I wouldn't mind hearing it again," she says, tucking a piece of hair behind her ear.

Glad to repeat my appreciation of her beauty, I say, "You're utterly bewitching. I'll be sure to remind you throughout the night. Ready to head down for dinner?"

"Yes. Please feed me. The fruit and snacks in my room are great, but I'd kill for a steak." Sadie closes her eyes as she half growls the last words.

Not able to help myself, I smirk down at her as I say, "I like a woman who can appreciate good meat."

"There are a lot of things I can appreciate," Sadie purrs back, dragging one nail down the front of my shirt.

"Like?" My voice is husky, my dick twitching at what she's insinuating.

"Getting in the elevator and actually sitting my ass down in a chair to finally get fed. Or do you prefer to just stand around and exchange innuendos until we both starve?" Sadie bats her eyelashes at me coyly.

I laugh. This woman is enchanting, and I can banter with her all day long.

"After you." I sketch a mock bow. "Allow me to appreciate your peachy ass."

Exaggerating the movement of her hips, she struts toward the door while I remain rooted to the spot as I take her in.

"Let's go, zooms," Sadie singsongs.

Wonderfully okay with doing her bidding, I race ahead to open the door to our suite and call the elevator.

It doesn't take long until we're enclosed in its cab, making our descent.

Taking advantage of a break in the sexual tension, I bring up what I've been contemplating while not preoccupied with thoughts of Sadie. "I was thinking that maybe tonight we could experiment with the distance limit. On the island I guessed it to be around a hundred yards, but I would like to confirm that theory here. I don't want to cause you any discomfort, so if you're not okay with it then we can just stick close to each other instead."

"I think it's a great idea. I'm sure you have a ton of work to do, people to meet, a hotel to run. I don't expect to be glued to your side while I'm here. You'd get so annoyed with me so quickly." She chuckles.

I drawl, "I can guarantee you that I wouldn't mind you glued to me." I give her a wink before I sober my tone and add, "But I want you to have your own space and make the most of your stay."

Sadie's brows scrunch up. "Thanks. I appreciate that." She gives her head a little shake as if to clear it. "Okay, how do you want to do this?"

"After we're done downstairs, I want you to take the elevator back up. If I feel the smallest tug, then I'll run up the stairs to reduce its effect on you," I explain, having given it some thought. It seems the most logical solution to move up in the elevator instead of down the street.

"Or we could stay on the phone with each other, and if I feel something, I can hit the stop button?"

I nod at her logic. "Or that. Beauty and brains."

Using our phones seems like a much easier method than running to a random floor.

Sadie rolls her eyes at me, but a smile plays around the corners of her mouth.

When we get downstairs, I stick my elbow out for her, just like I did on the island. "Milady."

She settles her hand easily in the crook of my elbow, like we've done this a thousand times before, and I marvel at how natural things feel between us.

I lead her to Liha, our best steak restaurant. This time she doesn't attempt to hide her dazzled expression.

I try to see it from Sadie's point of view, wondering what's fascinating her the most, but the way the amber glow from the low-hanging chandelier plays across her skin has me reaching for words. I'm momentarily struck speechless as I study her.

Her eyes are lit with excitement as they dart around the room, taking in each detail. From the low black leather armchairs to the high-backed tufted royal-blue velvet ones. From the burgundy-and-gold wallpaper and the framed photos covering the walls to the fully stocked bar at the center of the room.

I walk us over to a booth in the back that's always reserved for me, waiting for her to scoot in before I slide in on her other side.

"This place is beautiful. I've seen pictures online, but it's so much better in real life. The lighting, the music, the ambiance—it's perfect." Sadie's eyes keep roaming around, fingers playing with the sequins on her skirt.

She's such an interesting dichotomy, and I have a deep-seated desire to puzzle her out. One moment she's fully confident, but then when I say something nice, she gets a look of disbelief on her face, like she doesn't usually expect people to be considerate of her preferences.

I want, no, I *need* her to trust me. To feel safe enough to be herself around me.

"It's my favorite place to eat. I'd hoped you'd like it. You said you wanted the steak? How do you take it?" *Please say rare, please say rare, please say rare.*

"Rare. That's the only way to go," Sadie says without hesitation.

My heart just stopped and kick-started back to life, racing like a cheetah with its tail on fire. Could this woman be any more perfect for me?

I take a surreptitious breath in and respond casually, "We can agree on that. I only eat mine rare. Maximum flavor."

Choosing that moment to divert her attention, I signal the waiter over and order our steaks—my portion double hers. I don't know why the thought comes to me, but I'm pleased that she's comfortable with seeing blood. Maybe my dormant vampire genes are peeking out to appreciate her.

"Let's play a get-to-know-you game."

Sadie narrows her eyes at me. "I'm a bit hesitant to play another game with you when I'm distracted by good food."

"No wagers, no repercussions. Just rapid-fire questions," I reassure her.

I only want this to be fun, no heavy topics to put her on the back foot.

"How many do we each get?" She cocks her head at me, my gaze instantly drawn to her beautifully elegant neck.

I've never given necks a thought in my life. As a dhampir, I don't need or want blood. But why am I suddenly watching her pulse throb under a very thin layer of skin?

Blinking away my weird thoughts about Sadie's blood, I answer her question. "Let's do five tonight, five tomorrow, and so on. We'll keep them light tonight, and as time passes, we can choose to increase the intensity."

I like to pretend that I spontaneously came up with this idea now, when, in fact, I've been contemplating ways to get to know her better. Making this a game and starting out light should help build her trust in me, which has somehow become imperative.

Sadie nods in approval. "I like that. But let's each get the option to veto one."

"Done. First question. What's your favorite flower?" I waste no time in getting to know her.

Sadie's eyes widen and a laugh falls from her. It's a magical sound. I don't think I've heard her carefree laugh until now. I might just have to resort to doing crazy things to ensure she'll laugh like that more. Every day.

"That's what you want to know?" she asks through her laughter, clearly amused by my easy question.

"Is that your first question?" I taunt slyly.

"No!" she cries. "Peonies. I love peonies."

I take out my mental notepad and jot that down.

Keeping with the theme, I throw her another softball. "Favorite food?"

Her smile is wide and uninhibited. She's positively radiant like this. "Steak. You going to keep them this easy?"

I grin at her. "Yup. Fa—"

"My, my. Don't you two look all cozy here," Alexandra intones.

The evil woman stands next to our table, looking down at us with a sneer marring her harsh features. I was so wrapped up in the conversation that I wasn't paying attention to anything outside of Sadie. Again.

"What the fuck are you doing here? I told you you're not welcome in this building," I whisper yell at her, craning my neck to look for one of my hotel's discreet security guards.

The restaurant has such a calm atmosphere that I don't want to disturb any of the patrons with the drama that seems to follow Alexandra everywhere.

Alexandra tuts. "No need to get your panties in a twist. I was merely passing through and thought I'd say hi." She shrugs like it's not a big deal that she's trespassing.

My anger roils in my gut, threatening to spill over into a verbal lashing. Clenching my teeth to keep my fury contained, I grit out, "You don't just pass through my hotel. What are you really doing here?"

"I was just leaving," Alexandra says faux sweetly, turning and taking a step away. Holding a finger up, she stops and pivots to face us. "Oh, by the way, your father sends his regards. Enjoy your dinner, lovebirds," she singsongs as she walks away with a wave of her fingers.

"I'm so sorry. I'm going to get this sorted out. Tonight. I'll ask the staff to keep an eye out for her from now on," I apologize to Sadie.

Sadie shakes her head and places her hand on mine on the table. "It's okay. I'm more sorry for you. What can I do to help?"

I turn my hand to lace our fingers together. "I appreciate you, but there's nothing to do right now. I'll sort this out after dinner. For now, let's maybe try to get back to our game. I'd much rather be thinking about you than whatever scheme my father is cooking up."

I can feel my anger dissipating as I look into Sadie's beautiful eyes. Something about her calms me and excites me at the same time, something that makes my heart beat faster. I'm turning into such a sap for her, and I don't mind it one bit.

"You know, there are other ways to distract you too," Sadie

says seductively, a playful smirk pulling at the corner of her mouth.

"Let me guess, I've just got to 'beg' for it first?"

Sadie laughs. "Dammit, you knew where I was going with that."

Deciding to get us back on track, I admit, "I'm starting to read you pretty well. Now, favorite music?"

"I mostly listen to pop, but I like anything I can dance to." Sadie shimmies her shoulders to an imaginary beat, causing a huge smile to spread across my face.

My tongue toys with one of my canines. "I'd love to see some of your moves. Favorite drink?"

"For cocktails, I love a good piña colada. I also like white wine. I want to like red, but I think my taste buds are not quite sophisticated enough for that yet."

That makes me laugh. Her honesty is refreshing, even with the slight self-deprecation there at the end.

"Fair enough. I like that you know your preferences so well and can be honest about it. Final question. What do you look for in a male?"

"First of all, I don't go out *looking for* males. But if I had a preference, I'd say if you hit me with good banter, indulge my love for sparkly things, and give me some good D, I'll be the best thing that's ever happened to you."

I choke on my water and hit my chest with my fist, trying to process what she said.

"You thought I'd veto that question, didn't you?" A self-satisfied smile is firmly in place on her full lips.

"I underestimated the size of your lady balls. My bad," I croak out and take another sip of water. "You want your five questions?"

Sadie narrows her eyes at me as I anticipate her first question. "Favorite flower?"

I laugh again, and she joins in. My heart does a funny skip, and my stomach suddenly feels all weird. Is this what they mean when they say you've got butterflies?

"I guess I'm going to say peonies. Don't know much about flowers, but I'm now oddly invested in finding out what peonies look and smell like."

She beams at me. "Favorite food?"

"Are you going to throw all my own questions back at me?"

"Maybe." Sadie gives me a flirty smile, and I swear my eyes have hearts in them.

I let my eyes roam over her face, trying to memorize each feature and simultaneously figure out what it is about her that's making me addicted to her smiles.

"Tomorrow you're going to ask questions first, and then I'll throw them right back at you. Be warned," I tease.

"I'm ready for it. Now answer the question."

"I'm going to be boring and also say steak." I shrug unapologetically. "Looks like we're two peas in a pod."

"Music?" she asks slowly, stretching the word out like she's nervous to hear my answer.

"I wish I had a really cool answer for you, but I usually just listen to podcasts."

"Oh." Her lips turn down at the corners. "I guess preferring podcasts is better than having atrocious taste in music. You're not much of a dancer then, are you?"

"I'm not, but I think I'd be okay with watching you dance for me." I wink at her and instantly scold my eye for doing it. Again.

Sadie shakes her head, but I don't miss the faint smile she's trying to cover when she scratches her nose. "I've got two more. I'll keep this one easy, same as yours—favorite drink?"

"I do enjoy some top-shelf whiskey. I have a couple of brands at my place that I rotate depending on my mood."

I can't help but wonder what it would be like to have Sadie there with me. To sit out on the balcony at sunset, enjoying a good whiskey while watching the lights turn on across Vegas. The image warms something inside me, like a cold-blooded lizard basking in the warm desert sun.

Unaware of how long-term thoughts of her have become, Sadie asks, "Your place? Where do you live?"

"Ah, the final question. I've got a place in The Ridges. I'd love to show it to you sometime."

"I'd love to see it." Her smile is soft, genuine, and it ignites something deep in my soul.

The rest of the conversation is easy and the mood comfortable. There is no more blatant flirting, yet I feel more drawn to her with every minute, every smile that passes between us. She's smart as a whip, wonderfully kind, and incredibly funny.

She's the complete package.

I'm already lamenting that this is temporary. I wonder what it would take for her to be enticed to stay. Surely she wouldn't want to be saddled with a monster boyfriend who mostly works late hours. And to be honest, I don't know what I'd do in Kentucky.

Once our meal is done, I place her hand back in the crook of my elbow and lead her out to the lobby. I want to introduce her to more of my staff and show her where Pierce's office is.

Pierce is so important to the running of my everyday life and knows me well. If I'm not available, then I want Sadie to feel comfortable enough that she can contact him.

After knocking on his open door, I step inside, pulling Sadie in after me.

"Mr. Ülavere, Ms. Everly, good evening. How can I help you?" Pierce stands from behind his desk and inclines his head in a greeting.

"Hi, Pierce. I'm just showing Sadie around. I want her to know where your office is in case she needs something and is unable to reach me."

"I thought we agreed that you'll call me Sadie?" she playfully scolds him.

Pierce looks chastised, his hulking frame shrinking in on itself with a wince. Addressing Sadie, he says, "Sorry, Sadie. I'll keep that in mind. I have already reported your stay to the staff you might come in contact with. Don't be alarmed if you are greeted by name. But they'll most probably call you Ms. Everly." He winces again.

Sadie scrunches her nose up as she considers it. "You worry too much, Pierce. I just don't want to cause any hassles while I'm here."

His shoulders sag with relief as he extends his hand toward Sadie. "Please take my business card. You can call me if you need anything, even if I'm not on duty. "

"That's really kind of you, but I'm not going to bother you on your time off." Sadie lifts her hands in a friendly dismissal.

"It is no problem, Ms—Sadie," he corrects himself as he pushes the card into her hand.

She gives him a grateful smile.

The interaction between them makes my heart swell with contentment. Sadie is quickly becoming important to me, and to have her getting along with the people in my life just feels right.

"Mr. Ülavere, if you have a moment, I'd like to chat with you about some whales that came in last night," Pierce says, snapping me back to reality.

Daydreams of a life with Sadie evaporate with the sound of his deep voice.

Sadie looks at me, confusion dancing in her eyes as she mouths, "Whales?"

I grin at how odd that must sound to her. "It means high rollers," I explain. "A casino term you'll get used to." Turning back to Pierce, I ask, "Can you send an email with the information? Once I'm back in the suite, I'll attend to it."

"I will do that, sir. Um..." Pierce hesitates to speak, alerting me to the seriousness of what he wants to say.

"You can speak freely, Pierce. I've got nothing to hide from Sadie," I say, confused about what's got him so uncharacteristically stressed.

"Alexandra has been seen on the premises again. Security has been alerted and has eyes on her. It seems that she is moving toward the high-rollers area," he reports, confirming a theory about Alexandra that's been building in the back of my mind.

"Thanks, Pierce. I'll call you later to discuss this further. Please keep monitoring the situation."

Pierce gives me a stiff nod, and we say our goodbyes. I take Sadie by the elbow and steer her away.

We make a couple more rounds where I introduce her to some of the floor staff. Then I give her a quick tour around the casino.

When I try to take her to the shopping area, she digs her heels in and shakes her head. "Nope. Not going in that direction."

"Why not? Don't you like to shop?" I ask, confused.

I thought I had a pretty good read on her and her love for clothes.

"I love it, but the temptation would be too much. It's better if I just go back upstairs now."

Temptation? Is she worried about the cost of clothing?

Thinking I've figured out why she doesn't want to shop, I say brightly, "Choose something. It's on me." I think some of the clothes here would suit her really well. She seems to like the Vegas style, and I'd love to treat her.

Sadie crosses her arms over her chest. "I'm not a charity case."

"It's not charity. It's a gift. Maybe something sparkly," I try, making spirit fingers to indicate sparkles.

Sadie's eyes dart around as if searching for the right answer before shaking her head. "Thanks for the thought, but not today. This evening has been wonderful, and I don't want to ruin it with feelings of obligation."

The smile she shoots me is lackluster, the sheen in her eye from earlier now absent.

"Sadie, I'm sorry if I said the wrong thing. I just wanted to spoil you with something nice," I explain, unsure of what I said to offend her.

"It's really sweet of you, though I don't need anything." Her tone brightens as she rallies herself. "Let's go figure out this distance limit thing. I'm too full to be trying on clothes anyway."

She takes my hand and leads me back to the private elevator. Usually, I enjoy being the one leading her around, but I find myself not minding her taking charge. In fact, it intrigues me. Would she want to take charge in the bedroom too? I bet she'd love having me at her mercy. I think I'd like putting my pleasure in her promising hands.

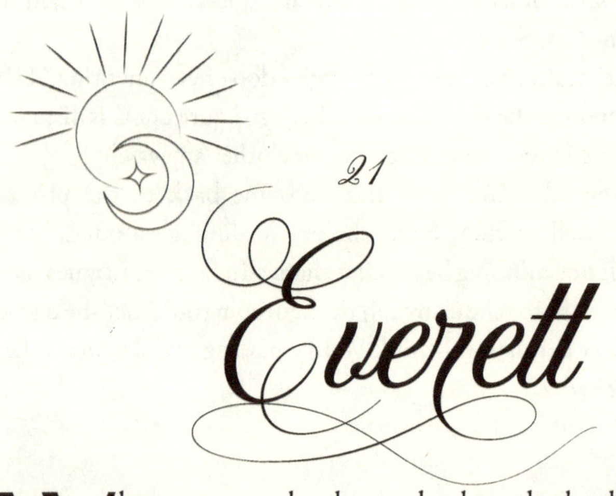

Everett

When we get to the elevator bank, we both take out our phones.

Sadie stares at me, disbelief creasing her brow. "You know what? I don't have your number. We haven't been apart since we met."

"You won't find me complaining about being close to you all the time. But I am complaining about not having your number," I say as I unlock my phone and hand it to her.

She gives me her phone, and I quickly put in my details, making sure the name I enter will be easy for her to find.

When she passes mine back, I laugh. "You saved yourself as 'sparkly princess'?"

"What? Don't you think it suits me?"

"I would've saved you as 'sparkly queen,'" I tell her without a trace of sarcasm.

She blinks at me. And just keeps blinking. I think I've broken her.

Just to be sure, I ask, "Are you okay? Need some mouth-to-mouth to restore your faculties?"

"Wouldn't you love to?" she asks, back to her normal self.

"Undoubtedly," I reply honestly.

The thought of her mouth on mine has crossed my mind too many times to count.

We both burst out laughing at how ridiculous the exchange is.

Once we're breathing normally again, Sadie asks, "Are you always this honest? This direct?"

"Actually, no. Only with you."

I take a moment to think on that and realize it's true. I've never been so forward with someone or so needy for their attention. I don't think I've found anyone interesting enough before to have me this thoroughly captivated.

"How about you, sparkles? Are you usually so direct with your... interest?"

Sadie shrugs. "I don't have a problem with speaking my mind, but I can truthfully admit that this is a new level for me."

"I feel special," I say, clutching my heart.

"You should," she replies dryly, then looks at her phone. "'Bet winner'? Really?"

"You know it's bound to happen. Want to watch me in the shower later and see what you're missing out on?" I waggle my brows.

"Not in your wildest dreams," she scoffs.

I can't seem to help myself as my filter disappears, and I utter, "Sweetheart, I promise you, you can't imagine how wild my dreams are when it comes to you."

Sadie sucks in a breath, completely caught off guard by my unrepentant candor. Indecision wars in her eyes, her mouth opening to say something, but whatever words she was about to say melt on her tongue with the ding of the elevator's arrival. Her shoulders deflate before she shifts back to her confident self and enters the elevator.

"I'm changing your name as soon as I'm upstairs. Better answer for now," Sadie mock threatens me as the elevator doors close.

A couple of seconds later, I answer Sadie's call while walking to the stairs. "Sparkles, I want to know what you were going to say before the elevator arrived."

"I wasn't going to say anything, zooms," she lies.

"Tell me when you reach floor twenty, please. And place your finger above the stop button, ready to press it the moment you feel discomfort," I instruct her, changing from flirty to serious mode. I don't want her to have the same bad experience she had on the island.

"I'm ready. Floor fifteen now." Sadie's nerves are evident in the quiver of her voice.

I try to reassure her, meaning my words. "I've got you. You're safe with me."

"I know, but I'm bracing myself anyway. Floor twenty." The strength in Sadie's voice is now almost gone, leaving her completely vulnerable.

I feel incredibly lucky that she's letting her guard down around me, and I'll do almost anything to keep her trust.

I infuse extra strength into my voice, a counterbalance to hers that she can take from. "Get ready."

My foot is on the first step, ready to run the moment she needs me.

"Twenty-five." Her quiver is stronger than before, but she's not even trying to hide her nerves now.

I bounce on my feet, anxiety swimming in my gut.

"Everett."

The phantom hook in my gut pulls me forward the moment she says my name.

"Stop the elevator, Sadie," I bark as I fly up the stairs. "What floor are you on?"

"Twenty-seven."

"I'm coming, Sadie. Hold on." This must be the fastest my feet have ever carried me before, the need to get to her quickening my strides.

Breathing hard, I exit onto the landing on the twenty-seventh floor. Sadie is waiting in front of the closed elevator doors.

"You really just ran up twenty-seven floors?" She gawks at me, eyes big, mouth agape.

I pant, "Are you okay?"

The image of her standing in the middle of the great room in Bertie's house, looking so forlorn, still haunts me. I never want to see her looking or feeling like that again. I have a new inherent need to guarantee her safety. Her happiness. The draw to her keeps getting stronger and stronger.

"I'm okay. Are you hurt?" Sadie asks in a soft voice, understanding the concern visible on my face.

There's no use in trying to hide it, it's too strong.

"Not hurt. Did you feel a tug like last time? Did the invisible tether move you? Hurt you?" My hands hover between us, wanting to reach for her body and inspect her myself, but not knowing if she'll welcome my touch.

"Not like last time. It felt more like a strong pull to you from deep in my body. I had an urge to get out and run to you," Sadie explains.

"I guess this time it was reversed for us. I'm glad you're okay, but let's not stretch that boundary again. I don't want you to experience that level of discomfort again."

It feels so unnecessary to inflict this on both of us. I'd rather just stick close together for the foreseeable future.

"That's really sweet. Thank you, but I'm totally fine. I'm more concerned about you having run up so many flights." Sadie gestures to my heaving chest.

"It's really fine. I work out a lot." I shrug, trying to pretend it wasn't a big deal. "I'll just count that as my cardio for the day."

"Work out? Really? I couldn't tell," Sadie says dryly.

Her sarcasm catches me so off guard that I reach out and tap her butt with a light spank.

"Oh," she moans.

I close my eyes and breathe deeply. I did not intend to spank her. It just kind of happened. But her responding moan is unexpected, and the burgeoning scent of her arousal fills my lungs.

"I'm sorry, sparkles. I didn't mean to do that. I seem to lack basic self-control when I'm around you."

"Don't apologize. That little swat was just threatening me with a good time."

I stab the button repeatedly to call the elevator again, and my brain belatedly registers what she's saying. "Threatening with a good time?"

"Oh, come on. Most women enjoy a good spanking. I've been dreaming of one but haven't had a man—or male—brave enough to give me *exactly* what I crave."

Praying for the elevator to hurry up so I can remove the enticing morsel of temptation from my sight before I give her a rightful spanking, I dare ask, "And what 'exactly' do you crave?"

"Nothing much. Just someone who can take charge, manhandle me, disrespect me a bit, spank me if I misbehave..."

A groan reverberates deep in my chest. I know she can hear it, and I'm sure she knows how much her words are affecting me.

Keeping my eyes closed, I thank the fates for placing this woman in my life. Her sexual preferences match mine perfectly. My hands curl into fists so I don't grab her and ravish her in front of an elevator.

And like the fates have heard my plea, the elevator dings with its arrival. I step inside first and quickly move to the back corner. Sadie follows and stands in the opposite corner closest to the door. Silent. She places her keycard against the panel that will allow the elevator to reach our floor.

I can't talk to her right now because my control is hanging on by a thread. I'm wound too tightly to even make a sound.

Only the quiet whirring of the machines as we ascend, and my labored breathing, are to be heard. The changing numbers of the floors on the elevator screen act as a countdown to the inevitable.

The silence stretches around us. Thick. Palpable with desire.

I need Sadie.

Tonight.

Now.

With a *ping*, the doors to our floor slide open.

The tension between Everett and me has been building since the island. Every day it gets stronger and stronger. With the addition of the little wager we have going on, someone is bound to snap soon. We're both riding the edge. But who will cave first?

I've been in a near-constant state of arousal since I met him. My attraction to him grows with every interaction. With Everett's wealth, insanely good looks, and magnetic personality, he feels so far out of my league. That he even reciprocates an iota of what I feel for him blows my mind.

I'm aware of our mutual attraction, our explosive chemistry, but once we fuck, it'll probably be out of his system, and then he'll move on. They all usually do.

I'm not kidding myself into thinking Everett would want me in a more serious way, no matter how charming he's been so far. My heart needs to stay safe behind the walls I've built because if I allow Everett in, I don't think I'd recover if he gets bored with me.

Most men find me a little "too much." I don't purposefully try to be, but I've been told I speak my mind a little too boldly, dress a little too provocatively, make jokes that are a little too crass. According to them, I'm there for a fun time, not a long time.

Despite not *needing* a male, I sometimes think it would be nice to be wanted for longer than the "fun" season. If I need to dim my sparkle to fit that mold, I might have to eventually do that. Maybe that's why I'm in Vegas—one last glitterfest.

I'll treat my stay in the city of sin as my final hurrah. I'll enjoy my sequined life fully, live as loudly and boldly as I want. When I have to leave here, I'll leave my sequins behind too. I'll conform.

Seems like a fair trade for steady companionship, maybe even one day a family.

But for the time being, I'll enjoy being unapologetically me. Dress in the most glittery outfits I own. Make the crass jokes. Drop my inhibitions. If Everett is keen to play, then I'm all in for as long as I'm here.

When the elevator doors slide open, I exit first, strutting down the long hallway to our suite. I glance back to see if Everett's coming, but he's not even looking up or acknowledging me. He's frozen to the corner of the cab, barely breathing, his gaze fixed on the ceiling.

Giving him the space I think he needs, I unlock the door and prop it open for him. I don't bother to turn on the lights as I head into the living room and drop down on the ornate oversized armchair to take my shoes off, then pad over to the floor-to-ceiling windows to admire the view. It's so unbelievably beautiful that I could stare at it forever.

"Sadie." My name is a plea.

I turn slowly. Everett is bracing himself in the doorway, his knuckles white from the pressure of his straining grip on both sides of the doorjamb.

Hanging his head between his shoulders, he looks to the floor when he speaks. "I might look like a man, but make no mistake, I am a monster. My senses are far keener than mere animals. So while you stand there, trying to appear as if you're not as affected as me, I can smell your cunt dripping with the need to know what I can do to it. Once your brain catches up with your needy cunt, just let me know, and I can show you what it's like to be ravaged by a dhampir."

I'm getting wetter with every word that comes out of his mouth. My thong is so soaked that my arousal is starting to drip down my inner thigh, over the tattoo I share with Everett. My heart rate picks up, a mirror to the throbbing pulse in my clit.

A whimper crawls up my throat and falls across my lips, making Everett's head jerk up.

His eyes lock on mine, his own breaths sawing in and out of his lungs, the wood creaking under the pressure from his hands.

"I can hear your quickening breath. I can see your dilated pupils. I can smell your wetness seeping through your panties. Now, why don't you be a good girl and let me taste to confirm you're as delicious as you smell? Let me touch you and sate that thirsty cunt."

"Yes," I breathe out.

In less than a blink of an eye, Everett is across the room. He holds himself back an inch from me, his body practically vibrating with restraint.

Breathing heavily, he fixes his nearly all-black eyes on mine. "I'm not going to beg. Do you want me to play with your pussy?"

"Yes" is all I manage to get out. Such an eloquent hussy suddenly, but he seems to have scrambled my brain, my pussy doing all the thinking for now.

Everett's gaze turns seductive. With an arrogant tilt to his lips, he asks, "Would you like my fingers, my tongue, or my cock?"

Oh, fuck. He can probably smell how much wetter I'm getting by the second. Would it be too forward to say all three? Maybe I should just choose one for now. But which one? My brain can't function when he's looking at me like that. I've never been given a choice like this before. Usually I'm just happy if I can make myself come while the guy takes care of his own pleasure.

"Mmm... it looks like all three of those options interest you. Should I start with my tongue and then proceed from there?"

"Yes. Three. Start. Tongue."

What are words even? Can I English? I feel hypnotized by this male, but I know that's not one of his powers. Definitely dickmatized, then.

In the next moment I'm lifted into the air. My bare back is pressed against the cool glass of the window, eliciting a hiss from me. Everett maneuvers me so my thighs straddle his broad shoulders and my skirt is shoved up to my waist. He grips my hips, fingers gloriously digging into the flesh of my ass.

Dipping his head, he noses at my clit through the fabric of my thong and licks up the center.

I moan at the sensation, my eyes closing of their own accord. Burying my fingers into his dark hair, I try to ground my body in some way while being so high in the air, at someone else's mercy.

I don't always enjoy being on the petite side, but being manhandled like this has been a fantasy of mine for a very long time. Everett's superior strength is an added benefit that takes my fantasy to new heights.

He keeps licking at my cunt over the fabric, alternating the broad strokes of his tongue with light nibbles along my pussy lips. He's ravenous, going at his task with full focus. The sounds coming from him are deliciously lewd.

My own mewls rise with each pass of his tongue, my pussy getting greedier, needing more.

Like he can read my mind, he carefully shifts his grip and lowers me down, my body sliding against his on its descent.

"I need you to remove this silly scrap of material between your legs so I can enjoy my dessert properly," Everett says hoarsely, his gaze feral.

"Okay."

One day I'll be capable of normal conversation again. But while Everett is taking charge of my body, it seems like I'm incapable of forming coherent sentences.

I'm about to remove my thong, but Everett scoops me up in his arms and speeds us over to his room, gently laying me down on his California-king bed. The bright lights from the Strip shine a kaleidoscope of colors into his room through the open curtains. The varied hues transform his white sheets into a live rainbow and highlight the hungry glint in his eye as he stares down at me.

Looking at this beautiful male, I'm in awe that he is so focused on bringing me pleasure. I've never had a guy *want* to do this. I've always been the one who had to give head while getting myself off, most of them being of the opinion that eating pussy is beneath them.

"I'm going to remove your panties now." Everett's voice is like gravel, his breathing labored as he studies me.

I just nod, still unable to form full sentences, and lift myself up onto my elbows so I can see him better.

He glides his hands up from my ankles, almost reverently, taking his time to explore the feel of my skin under his rough palms, all the way up my thighs. When his hands reach my thong, he slides his fingers under the thin strip of material on each side and slowly drags them down. His eyes follow the unhurried descent of the panties, his breaths growing heavier the closer they get to him.

Hooking them off my ankles one by one, Everett brings them to his nose and inhales deeply with his eyes locked on mine. With a smirk, he tucks the panties into his pocket.

"Sadie. You have no idea how mouthwatering your scent is. It's driving me crazy. The little taste I got back there was just a tease. I need more. "

Oooh, I have superpowered horny juices, good to know.

"I need you to spread your legs for me now so I can lick every drop of your delicious cream. Think you can do that for me, sweetheart?"

"Yes." I wish my voice sounded as confident as I want it to sound, but it still astounds me that he's actually enjoying my smell, my taste.

I step my legs out, exposing my pussy to him.

Everett runs his tongue along one canine, then growls, "More."

I widen them up to the edge of discomfort, putting myself fully on display for him.

"What a beautiful cunt you have. It's dripping for me. Are you going to make a mess of my bed, sparkles? Let the scent of your arousal permeate my room so I can smell you for days after?"

Yes, most definitely, if he keeps talking like that.

But he's also reminding me that this is just a one-off thing. Just for tonight we're going to have a moment of weakness and enjoy each other. I shouldn't forget that this is temporary. I'm going to force myself to lock all these mushy feelings away. I'll reevaluate them when I'm long gone from here.

With my mind firmly in the game now, I wrench myself out of the trance I was in and play along.

"Are you just going to stare at it, or you actually going to put your tongue to work and make me scream?"

Everett looks elated at my taunt and, on the next breath, dives forward. He moves his mouth to my inner thigh, right to the new tattoo, and gives it a tender kiss.

"You have no idea how pleased I am that I get to share this mark with you. The fates were awfully kind to bind us together, for however long they want. But having you here, in my bed, is a fucking privilege." Everett keeps his mouth over the tattoo as he speaks, only making eye contact with me on the final words.

With one last press of his lips to the tattoo, he grabs me by the back of the knees and shoves my legs up, baring me obscenely to his wolfish gaze. And it's like something snaps in him.

Everett attacks my cunt like a man starved. Eating me sloppily, voraciously, no finesse whatsoever. It's almost as if he's the one who can't keep a cool head right now.

He places open-mouthed kisses on my pussy, from my entrance to my clit. The scrape of his stubble is a wonderful contrast to the smooth, wet heat of his tongue. With his tongue, he traces circles around my nub, making them smaller with each pass, applying more pressure until I'm a squirming, whimpering mess.

My arousal drips from my pussy, down my crack, onto the bed.

I grab his hair and place his mouth where I need him, wantonly grinding my hips into him. Everett closes his lips around my clit and sucks. The escalating cries that fall from my lips are obscene. I'm so close.

Right as I think I'm going to explode, he eases his mouth off my clit, eliciting a whimper from me at the loss. "Nooo, don't stop."

"I'm only getting started. The sounds of your pleasure are like music to my ears. I don't want this to end too soon. Now, let's see how loud you can scream for me," he says into my pussy, darkened gaze intent on me.

He gives a light nip to my inner thigh, right over the tattoo, before licking a broad stroke up my pussy. He moves from my clit down to my puckered hole where no one has ever been, letting his tongue trace around the rim, mapping all my most intimate parts.

I gasp at the new sensation.

"Has anyone ever touched you here, sparkles?"

"No." It doesn't even occur to me to lie right then.

"We'll have to explore that another time."

Another time? Like he's planning for more than tonight? A girl can dare to hope.

His tongue resumes its exploration and moves up my pussy, closer to where I need him. But instead of focusing on my clit, he shifts to my entrance and shoves his tongue into it. Firming his tongue, he moves it in and out, fucking me with it as I moan unashamedly.

My breasts feel heavy, my nipples hard points straining against the fabric. I move one hand from his hair to my breast, teasing my nipple, rolling and plucking it.

Everett sees this and redoubles his efforts, his hands moving down the backs of my thighs, my flesh likely bruising with his delicious grip. The sounds coming from him are broken, beastly groans of pleasure.

With his focus fully shifted to my clit, he closes his lips around it again and pulls on it with heavenly suction.

I'm so close that my muscles start to lock and tingles race down my spine, but I need something more to send me over that final edge.

My hand leaves my breast and moves aimlessly on the bedspread, unknowingly searching for that final element, settling in Everett's soft hair once again.

With both hands, I push his head down into my pussy as my hips roll into his face, wanting, needing just a final push. I'm so close, teetering on the edge, my breaths coming in short gasps, climbing in a crescendo with my racing heart.

Suddenly, there's a wonderful pinch of pain on either side of my clit, and I tip over.

"Everett!"

My eyes are closed in ecstasy as my legs tremble, my spine curving, my pussy fluttering.

The best orgasm of my life. Transcendent.

When I start coming down from my high, I gaze at Everett through heavy-lidded eyes, my heart rate gradually slowing down. I'm completely sated but somehow hungry for more, ready to bring him as much pleasure as he's given me.

The look on Everett's face, though, isn't one I'd expect to see. Shock and something akin to horror mar his features. His brows are knitted, his mouth gaping open, his chest heaving.

My drunk haze begins to clear as it registers his expression, and my eyes catch sight of something that most definitely wasn't there before.

Long, sharp, glinting in the light...

"Everett, did you just grow fangs?"

His darkened eyes widen, and he slowly lets go of my legs, lifting a shaky hand to inspect his canines. In a blink he's standing in front of the mirror, baring his teeth at his reflection.

He turns to me with an apologetic look and speaks with a hand clamped over his mouth. "Sadie, you are perfect, a queen. But I need to—I'm so sorry—I'll be right back."

Everett runs out of the room, the door shutting behind him with a soft *click*.

And I'm left alone, half-naked on his bed, heart still pounding, readjusting my expectations of the evening. Of him.

23

Everett

Sadie was pure perfection—her scent, her taste saturated my senses and had me on the cusp of losing control. And what a beauty she was when she let herself lose control and screamed my name. That sight alone almost made me come undone.

I feel absolutely horrid leaving her there like that on my bed, still drunk on lust, but I had no other choice.

I have *fangs*.

My canines have always been elongated, but they've never descended like this. I know there's something unique between Sadie and me. This, however, takes it to a whole new level.

When I tasted her cunt, it was pure bliss. I couldn't get enough and felt myself turning feral, needing more. The desire to consume her grew stronger and stronger, increasing with every lick.

It was like I could sense her blood pumping through her body, her heartbeat a siren call to my basest being, compelling me to take more.

I didn't understand what my inherent nature was driving me to do... until I did it.

Right before her climax, she gripped my hair as she rolled her hips into my face, driving her delectable cunt closer, letting me devour her.

I don't know how it happened, but my teeth nicked her. Right next to her clit.

A drop of her blood touched my tongue, and it was like I finally believed in heaven.

For a moment I was transported to a whole other realm, until I realized that it was her blood.

I took from her without her consent.

I didn't expect to taste blood at that moment, and I was horrified at myself for losing control.

The taste of her cunt was incredible, but the taste of her blood was ambrosia.

I had to wrench my head away, not fully understanding what was happening.

Until she pointed out my fangs.

The moment I saw my reflection in the mirror, I knew I had to get out of there before I did something I couldn't take back.

I wanted more.

Needing guidance and not knowing who else to turn to, I make for the fire escape and call my best friend. He answers after the first ring.

"Everett."

"Bertie," I sigh, lowering myself onto a step.

"What has happened?"

"How can you tell?" I rest my elbows on my knees and let my head hang forward, propping it against the hand not holding my phone.

"I've been your friend for eighteen years. You don't call unless something extreme has happened. In light of the recent events with the women, I can only assume this has something to do with them." He makes a pretty good point.

"You'd be right to assume that. But it's actually more of a *me* thing," I admit.

I hear him shuffle some papers and a door closing. "Explain."

"I've got fangs," I state flatly, appreciating that Bertie wants to get straight to the point.

"As in vampire fangs?"

"Yup."

"When did they appear?" Bertie's oddly unfazed by my admission.

"Just now." I wince, Sadie's beautiful face etched with shock clear in my mind.

"I'm going to need more than that. But this doesn't surprise me." Bertie's calm is having the opposite effect on me.

"No?! I'm fucking freaking out over here, Bertie. I was with Sadie, in the… bedroom, and they just suddenly… appeared." I try to calm my frantic tone.

"Anything you can think of that triggered them to descend?"

"I don't particularly want to talk about Sadie to you, but yeah. Her scent and taste kind of overwhelmed me, yet I wanted more," I confess, pulling at my hair, hating how helpless I feel right now.

Bertie's next question startles me. "Could you sense her blood?"

"Yeah, you could say that," I choke out. "Why?"

How could he have guessed?

"This makes sense to me. I have a theory, and this is a step closer to confirming it," he says, telling me something while not telling me anything at all.

I've forgotten how good he is at avoiding hard conversations until he's ready for them himself with all the facts he needs.

"Care to explain?" I ask slowly, rubbing at the stubble on my jaw.

"Not quite yet. I just returned from the library with new resources and will focus today's research around the theory you have just validated."

I'm sure he's probably holed up in his study to get as much research done as fast as possible. Bertie's sense of duty has always weighed heavily on him.

"You're not even going to give me a hint?" I ask with disbelief apparent in my voice.

"I will say that you should not be alarmed if more vampiric traits surface. If you aren't one-hundred-percent confident that you can regulate your new urges, then it would be better to have some space as an extra measure of security. For her safety. You have sworn an oath to protect," he reminds me.

I sigh and stretch out my legs. "That's partly why I ran out. I want her to feel safe, and the sudden appearance of fangs might freak her out more than they did me."

"Will *you* be okay?" The kindness in his tone calms my racing heart a tad.

"Yeah, I'll be. Thanks," I say, my voice hoarse. "I'll let you get back to it. Let me know if you find anything, please. If there's any way I can help from over here, I'd be more than happy to."

"Thanks, Everett. I appreciate that." Bertie clears his throat. "I'll call you if I find anything certain."

Before he can hang up, I quickly tack on, "Florence and you getting on well?"

Bertie coughs. "It's fine. She's fine," he says quickly.

My eyebrows shoot up my forehead, curiosity needling me. "Should I ask?"

"Better if you don't."

That piques my interest even more. But I'll leave it for now and ask him next time he calls.

"Got it. Talk soon, then."

"Fates be with you," Bertie replies, and I can't help but think how apt that greeting is.

I remain sitting on the step after the call and trace my finger over a fang. They're gone. Just my normal elongated canines remain. What does this all mean?

As I start contemplating everything that's happened tonight, it dawns on me that leaving Sadie all splayed out on my bed might have given her the wrong impression.

I'm not okay with that.

Furious with myself, I shove all my confusing emotions aside, Sadie—and fixing whatever misunderstanding I may have caused—my sole focus.

I get up and rush back to my room, but she's not there. Her delicious scent remains embedded in the fabric of the room, the only evidence that she was there at all.

Gathering my wits, I stalk over to her room and knock lightly.

She doesn't answer. But I also don't expect her to.

"Sadie. Can I come in?" I ask tentatively.

No answer. I know she's not asleep because I've only been gone a few minutes.

"Sparkles, let me in. Please." I'm not above begging at this point.

"It's open." Sadie's tone is wary, and I remind myself that it's my fault.

I made her doubt how perfect that was, how perfect *she* is. I have zero regrets about everything that's happened, up until I fled, but I thought it was a smart choice at the time.

Her room is almost pitch-dark, the blackout curtains drawn with only a sliver of light peeking through from outside.

Sadie's curled up in the white lounge chair by the window in an oversized white T-shirt. Her legs are drawn up tight, arms wrapped around them, as she leans her head on her knees and stares at the wall.

I stop just inside the door, sensing she's not quite ready for me to get in her personal space.

In a gentle voice, I plead. "Sadie, please look at me. Let me explain what happened. Please."

"Don't worry about it. I think it's better if we just give each other some space until I leave." She's still not looking at me as she says this, and my heart squeezes uncomfortably in my chest.

"Yeah, that's not happening."

Her head snaps up, and her eyebrows furrow in shock. "Excuse me?"

"You see, wanting space, that's going to be a problem for me." I shrug one shoulder, feigning a cool exterior.

"Why?"

"Because I like you," I state.

I'm done playing games, making wagers. This woman is amazing, and she deserves the straightforward truth.

"What?"

I walk deeper into the room and turn on the bedside light so I can see her better, so she can see me better. See how sincere I am in my apology and my confession. I move closer and sit down on the footstool in front of her, leaning forward with my elbows on my thighs to catch her eyes.

"I like you. I want to spend more time with you. Get to know you. I'd like you to give me a chance. But if you don't want to, I'll respect your decision. Maybe just think about it first, please." I wince on the last word, hoping it doesn't sound too desperate.

"If you like me, how can you just make me come and then run out? Did I taste bad or do something wrong?" She's trying to sound strong, but her bottom lip slightly quivers, giving her away.

I shift forward and take her hands into my own, careful to keep my touch light and tender. I'm grateful that she's letting me hold them.

"Sadie, you're magnificent. Your taste is incredible, better than I ever could have imagined. It's fucking ambrosia. If you'd let me, I'd like to eat you out at least once a day."

"Pft, no one likes pussy that much," she scoffs.

"Your pussy was made for me. But more than that, I felt honored that you shared your body with me. Can I explain what happened?"

"Honestly, I'm scared to know what could have spooked you that bad that you left me half-naked on your bed, my pussy still pulsing, your face wet with my desire, before you were out the door. I've been ghosted before, but even this was a first for me."

"I'll truly regret leaving like that, but I had to before—" I cut myself off, afraid what I was going to say would probably have her running for the hills or as far as the bond will allow her.

"Before?" She prompts, eyebrows raised.

"Before I bit you." I shrink back, disgusted with myself.

"Come again?" She shakes her head as if she didn't hear me correctly.

"So, the thing is"—I take a deep breath and ready myself to admit out loud what I haven't been brave enough to admit to myself yet—"I think you're awakening my vampire side. I've never felt any kind of cravings for blood, but my fangs grew suddenly, and I didn't know, and then they accidentally nicked you, and I tasted a drop of your blood, and it was the most decadent thing I've ever tasted, and I wanted more." I ramble that out all in one breath, hoping she caught some of it but also kind of not.

"Uh..."

"Yup." I pop the *p*.

"Are you a vampire now? Do you need to drink blood?"

"I don't think so, but there's something about *your* blood that calls to me. Everything about *you* calls to me. And I think it's connected to the tattoos or to the fates. I called Bertie, and he's still researching, but he's not surprised by my sudden 'interest' in your blood. Am I freaking you out?"

"Weirdly, no. It's actually a little flattering that I made you feral," she says smugly.

"I also need to clarify, it's not *just* your blood that has spiked my interest in you. Since that first moment I saw you in the clearing, I was captivated. You're the most exquisitely beautiful woman I've ever seen. You're smart, funny, witty. Your confidence is hot. I like that you know who you are and that you dress in clothes that make you happy. I know it's early days, and this seems like a lot, but I would love to get to know you better. Take you on dates. I had a great time at dinner earlier, and every moment spent with you so far has been fun." I infuse as much passion as I can into my words. I want her to know how much I value her as *her*, not for whatever is happening with her blood and my sudden cravings. "What do you say? Will you give us a chance?"

"Good thing I like you too, otherwise that speech would've been a little embarrassing." Her smile is small. Gentle.

My chest swells with pride and fuzzy feelings because I'm going to get to date this magnificent woman.

"I think we attempted things a bit backward. Usually it's a confession first, then a kiss, then oral, and so on. But somehow we skipped over everything, and I got to start with your delicious cunt."

"Guess we're special like that. I don't like following any set rules anyway. And the oral was kind of amazing, so I'm not going to let the order bother me."

"Good to know. I'd like to kiss you now. Would that be okay?" My nerves are evident in the deep swallow that follows my question.

"Yeah, better make it a good one." Her face softens, and her smile is playful.

Accepting her challenge, I pull her out of her seat and sweep my hands up her arms, over her shoulders and along her collarbone, then up her neck. I cradle her face between my hands and slowly lean down.

The first pass of my lips over hers is a delicate caress. Two, three more passes as she softens against me. I move one arm to her lower back and draw her up against my chest, her arms wrapping around me, body melting into mine, never breaking our kiss.

My tongue peeks out in a question, and she parts her lips, inviting me in. The kiss is soft and languid as our mouths move together, our tongues twining, playful.

This kiss is better than I could have imagined. She tastes so sweet and matches each of my movements with her own.

I move my hand to the nape of her neck, weaving my

fingers through her long strands as I grip her hair lightly and direct her head back so I can deepen the kiss.

Her mouth opens wider on a gasp, and I plunge deeper, stronger, as we meet each other stroke for stroke in a steady rhythm.

Our kiss turns greedy, her sweet moans in perfect harmony with my voracious groans. Her scent wraps around me like the sweetest embrace.

Before it can lead to more, I start slowing down, letting the kiss turn lazy with soft strokes and gentle presses of lips. I bring my hand down from her hair and cradle her jaw once again.

So much has happened tonight, and I want to do things right from now on. Show her I'm serious about dating her, getting to know her, even with my vampiric traits bubbling to the surface.

With one last brush of our lips, I kiss the corner of her mouth, then wrap her in my arms. She hugs me back, causing my breath to shudder out of me in pure pleasure.

Holding her like this just feels right.

Like something momentous has fallen into place, and I can't wait to figure out what it is.

But for now, I'm going to say good night, go to my room, and relive all the events from today.

I move my mouth to her forehead and place a soft kiss there. Letting my lips linger, I speak against her skin. "Good night, Sadie-queen. Sweet dreams. Get ready to be wooed tomorrow."

With one final press of my lips to her forehead, I slide my arms away. My racing heart keeps me company on the way to my room as I start making plans to get Sadie to fall in love with me.

24

Sadie

This time when Everett leaves me in a bedroom, my heart is sprinting for a whole different reason. That kiss was the most phenomenal kiss of my life. But more than that, his words, how much he likes me and wants to get to know me, have my brain racing with possibilities and my stomach fluttering with butterflies.

I have to call Cece to tell her about it.

I get my phone out and see she sent me a message earlier.

Cece: Call me!!! Tell me everything!!

Needing to hear my sister's voice and see her face, I click on the video call icon next to her name.

"Dede!" my sister answers brightly, her pretty smiling face filling the screen.

"Cece!" I match her enthusiasm.

"I'm so glad you called. I need to know how it all happened. How did you see him naked? Did he look *that* good? Have you done more? Tell me everything!" Cece fires all the questions out in one breath, making me grateful that I called her.

"Whoa, slow down," I laugh. "Let's have some conversation foreplay first before we get to good stuff."

She lets out a frustrated huff, then says, "Fair. But just so you know, I'm not really into edging. I'm waiting on pins and needles for the main event. But let's start with Vegas. How's the city?"

Relieved that I get to work up to the juicy part, I tell her, "The city is as bright and colorful as I'd hoped it would be. My glitter-loving self fits right in. How about where you are? How's Germany?"

Cece nods and tucks a piece of hair behind her ear. "It's good. But you should see the house, it's a dream."

"Cece, you've got to give me more than that. Is he treating you well?" I ask sternly, ready to fly to Germany if she needs me. I'd give Adelbert a good talking to if he's not treating my sweet sister as she deserves to be treated.

"He's doing his best. He's very busy and is locked in his library most of the day. I think the pressure of trying to fix the whole tattoo thing is really hard on him."

I get what she's saying, because everyone is kind of relying on Adelbert right now. But I want her to be happy there. Maybe I was hoping he'd be trying a bit harder to make her comfortable.

I give Cece an understanding smile. "You're way too kind for him. How are you staying busy?"

"You know, enjoying nature, walking around outside, within a hundred-yard perimeter obviously. He mapped it out for me." Cece's expression shifts to one of excitement as she leans closer to the camera. "Dede, it's so beautiful here, it reminds me of that dream I had of the woman dancing in the meadow, the one that I embroidered."

My skin tingles with what that could possibly mean. "After all the magical things that have happened, I wouldn't be surprised if it's actually a real place there and you were meant to find it. Can you show him pictures of the embroidery piece and see if he recognizes it?"

"Oh, I don't want to be a bother. He's really busy." Her phone lowers a fraction, and her shoulders slump forward.

"Florence," I warn, raising my eyebrows.

"Sadie," she mimics my tone and expression.

I keep my tone stern as I say, "You are worthy of more than just his time. So if you have a question, just go ask it."

I want my sister to ask for what she needs, to value herself the way I value her.

"I'll try asking soon, okay?" She gives me a wan smile. "Now, tell me, what's happening over there?"

"Well..." I start.

Cece's eyebrows shoot up, and her eyes round into saucers.

"Oh my goodness, did you guys *fuck*?" she whispers the last word.

I love my sister. She can have such a crass mouth underneath that sugary goodness, but she's nervous about showing that side of herself to other people.

"We didn't fuck, exactly. But he went down on me, and I swear I felt my soul leave my body. I've never come so hard." My giddiness over even just mentioning what happened tonight has got my shoulders doing a little shimmy.

"Yes! I knew all that chemistry was going to lead somewhere." Her delighted smile is all teeth.

I feel myself go a bit shy as I say softly, "He also told me that he likes me."

Cece scoffs, and a line forms between her brows. "What's not to like about you? Of course he was going to fall for you."

"No one is saying anything about falling." I shake my head. Surely she's overestimating his feelings for me.

"Yet." The furrow in her brows is replaced by a confident arch as a smug grin tugs at her lips.

"Cece..."

"Sadie. That male does not strike me as someone who'll just say something like that if he didn't mean it. What's got you hesitant?" She makes a good point.

"I don't know," I lie.

"You do. Tell me. I'm your big sister, let me help you fight your battles, even if they're all in your head and with yourself."

Well fuck, she's right. I don't want to admit this out loud, but if there's one person who will hear me out, judgment free, it's Cece.

"What if he likes me, and I like him back, and then Adelbert finds the fix, and then he grows bored with me without the magical link and sends me back to Kentucky by myself, but... my heart... remains in Vegas?" I try to rush the words out but stumble over the last few, admitting them out loud too hard for me.

"Oh, Dede. But what if it all works out? What if you both start liking each other, and it's real and strong? What if he asks you to stay?" she reasons in a gentle voice.

I close my eyes as I admit with a sad grimace, "He won't."

"Why not?" Cece asks in a sober tone.

"They never do. I'm the 'fun' girl. Guys grow bored of my 'too much-ness.' Everett says he's interested now, but I know it's just a matter of time before he reaches his limit and moves on to someone less... 'me.' I'm not trying to be insecure about it, but it's happened before. More than once." I'm ashamed to tell her all this, but I know my sister will understand me.

"Can I tell you what I saw on the island?" She moves to a new spot in the room she's in, repositioning her phone so I can see more of her.

"Please." My voice is small. I need all the reassurance I can get.

"That male was in a room with ten women, yet he never looked at anyone but you. His eyes were fixed on you the entire time. Like a magnet. I say you should be brave and give things a shot between you two."

"Yeah?"

"Definitely. How long do you have until school starts back up again? Maybe give it a proper go until then, then you can decide if you can make things work long distance or find another way."

My heart drops into my stomach, sinking to the lowly pit

it deserves to live in. Cece is such a good sister, and I haven't even shared the news with her.

"Oh, um… about school… There were some budget cuts… and I got pink-slipped," I mutter.

Cece's brows furrow. "Pink-slipped?"

"Oh, yeah. It means my position was cut. So I'm… um… technically unemployed. I sent my résumé out to a bunch of schools, but I'm still waiting to hear back," I confess, and flinch back from the hurt on her face.

"Sadie! Why didn't you tell me? I'm so sorry, it must be so stressful for you. Oh my goodness, what about our trip? If you told me, we could've canceled and saved that money." Cece rants at me, concern pitching her voice high.

I shrug and explain gently, "That's exactly why I didn't tell you. I wanted to go on the trip with you. I wanted it to be something special for the two of us. We also booked our tickets while I still had a job. Besides that, there was just something about the trip that made me feel like I shouldn't cancel it." My words are slow with guilt at having kept this from her, but I'm confident now that it was the right decision.

Cece takes a deep breath in and releases it on a slow exhale. "I know what you mean, I had the same feeling about going on this trip. Do you think it has anything to do with the males and the whole situation we've found ourselves in now?"

I nod and admit, "I'm starting to think that way."

"Just putting this out there, but if you ever want to consider trying something different, this could serve as a great opportunity to explore your options."

Swallowing hard, I can't quite keep eye contact with her as I say, "I've never enjoyed teaching as much as I should have. Don't get me wrong, the kids are great, but it's not something that brings me joy."

Cece tilts her head and asks, "Why did you choose to study it? I honestly thought you wanted to be a teacher."

I take a long breath in, readying myself to confess the biggest thing I've kept from my sister. In a voice barely above a whisper, I say, "It seemed like a stable job with a reliable income. I just wanted to have a safety net for us. Mom is off doing her own thing with Patrick, and as an adult, I don't want to bother her. Cece, you're such an incredible artist. I wanted to have that financial security so that you'll have more freedom to freelance. That if there was a tough month, you could count on me to help you out."

Tears fill Cece's eyes, escaping over the brim, and run down her cheeks. With a quaking voice, Cece says, "I'd *never* ask you to do that. I'm supposed to be the one taking care of you."

Wishing I could wipe her tears away, I ball my free hand into a fist. "I know you'd never ask, that's why I did it," I mutter, my voice choked with tears.

"Oh, you silly goose," Cece chastises me lightly, wiping at the tears with the back of her hand. "You know I'd never accept your money."

"I know." I laugh wetly around the word. Sniffing, I add, "And your business is so successful, you don't need anything from me. Don't worry, the irony is not lost on me."

"Well, now is the time to reassess what you want to do. You're only twenty-four. Maybe the universe is conspiring to set you on a new course," she says, ever the optimist.

All the tension I've been carrying with me for years seeps from my body, my limbs tingling with warm gratitude for my sister. "You're the best sister, you know that?"

Eyes glassy, Cece steels her voice. "Sisters by blood."

With a full heart, I reply, "Friends by choice."

"By the way, have you talked to Mom at all?"

We're not super close to our mom, but we see her every now and then. She got remarried after our father died and is currently living her best life with her new husband, Patrick.

"I sent her a message to say we're doing good, but I didn't tell her we're not in the Caribbean anymore."

Patrick and Mom frequently take trips, so we don't have to worry about her popping by our place to see us.

"Me neither," Cece says. "They're traveling somewhere for the next week, I think maybe the Grand Canyon, so she won't be looking for us. If we're going to be away for longer than that, then we'll have to come up with some sort of explanation."

I grin and nod in agreement, happy our mom has her own fulfilling life and won't be too concerned about us. "I think she won't worry too much. If she heard I was in Vegas, she'd probably just think I'm here to dress up and party. And you in Germany also kind of makes sense. She might think you went there for artistic inspiration."

"Good point." Cece giggles. "I'll just continue to be vague if she messages."

"Let me know if you tell her anything specific that I should know about."

"Will do." Cece peeks over the phone toward something behind the screen. "I've got to run. Adelbert is looking for me."

"I'm really glad we were able to chat. I'm happy you're okay over there," I say sincerely. Narrowing my eyes, I add, "Will you let me know if I should call Adelbert and give him a talking to?"

"That won't be necessary, but I'll keep the option in my back pocket, okay? Now you go and give Everett a real chance. Think about your future. Lower those walls you've built around your heart. Be brave," she preaches, pointing her finger good-naturedly at me.

"I'm going to try my best. And you go and speak your mind. Also be brave." I return the same gesture.

"Love you, sis."

"Love you too."

I exit our chat and lie back on the bed.

She made some good points. I can't always wait for the other shoe to drop. Living like that is stressful.

Starting now, I'm lowering my walls. Maybe not quite all

the way yet, but enough to see if there's potential for something special. It definitely felt like there was much more than a spark today. The way we teased, played, the way he asked questions and got to know me.

I don't want to sabotage myself or anything that could develop between us.

Firming my resolve, I climb into bed with a smile on my face, hopeful for what tomorrow may bring.

25

Everett

As my body stirs awake, I breathe in deeply, a contented sigh slipping past my smiling lips. Despite sleeping alone, Sadie's decadent scent still lingers in the room and wraps around me like a comforting embrace.

This. This is how I want to wake up every morning. But not just with her scent.

I want her tucked into my side, arms wrapped around me, her head on my chest, her thigh straddling mine, her hair spread out on my pillow.

The vivid image has my morning wood straining harder, begging my hand to find release. But I'm holding out.

When I got to my room last night, I started making calls and putting plans in motion, delaying hotel business. I'm trusting my staff to deal with all the daily admin while I focus on Sadie.

She's more important.

I didn't mean to eavesdrop, but my vampire hearing picked up Sadie's video call with Florence. I thought about putting on my headphones but hesitated when I heard what they were talking about. And I don't regret listening in.

Not when it's given me a clearer understanding of how Sadie thinks.

I'll do anything to prove myself to her. To let her feel that her heart is safe with me.

I want her to trust me.

To fall in love with me.

To stay.

With some extra pep in my step, I hit the shower and get ready for the day.

I can hear Sadie in her room listening to music, the sound dull as it's probably coming through headphones. It gives me time to make her coffee and arrange things around the suite.

By now I've learned to perfect her iced caramel latte, and I add a dollop of whipped cream on top. Coffee in hand, I head to her room.

The music is louder but still muffled here, and she doesn't hear my knock. Deciding to risk it, I open the door quietly.

The sight greeting me has a broad grin stretching across my face, crinkling my eyes. My heart takes off at a gallop once again, and I place my free hand on my chest to try to keep it in place.

She's in front of the mirror in her oversized T-shirt from last night, makeup brush in hand, holding it as a microphone as she lip-synchs and dances along to a song on her headphones. That's why she didn't hear me when I knocked.

Watching her move her hips and dance along to the choreography of the song is spellbinding. The bright morning sun shines on her like a spotlight in the all-white bedroom. Before I can stop myself, I feel my own hips start to sway to the beat.

When the choreography changes and she does a cute little butt wiggle, I know I'll do anything to keep her.

To make her mine.

Realizing she's still unaware of my presence, I open the door wider and knock loudly. I thought she'd scream or at least be startled, but she throws me a smirk and a wink over her shoulder.

"Wondered how long you were just going to stand there and stare," she says smugly as she moves the headphones to lie around her neck.

"You knew I was here?" I ask, surprised, taking a step into the room.

Sadie keeps moving her hips to the faint beat coming through the headphones. "I'm not sure how long you were standing there, but that smile on your face was very satisfying, and I wanted to see if it would stay there. So I kept dancing and let you enjoy the show."

"Ten out of ten," I praise. "Would love to see it again."

"It's obviously a very effective song. You looked—no, stared—even without me being all done up," she says proudly.

"You're beautiful, with or without makeup. The sexiest thing is when you're comfortably you, whether in a glittery dress or a plain T-shirt. It's one of the most attractive qualities about you, that you can unapologetically be yourself and dress in clothes that make you happy," I confess, my face and voice earnest.

I don't want her to doubt me, so I'll be honest and straightforward until she understands that I meant what I said last night.

Sadie tilts her head and studies my face. "I think you really mean that."

"I do." I hold her coffee out toward her. "Now, come take your coffee and head to the living room, I have a little something for you."

It's so hard to be cool when I'm actually sweating bullets. I hope she likes what I did.

"Extra whipped cream! Thank you." She takes a sip and beams at me.

Stretching onto her tiptoes, she plants a kiss on my cheek.

I swear fireworks go off around me, in me, my heart filling to the brim, my stomach doing fanciful cartwheels.

And all that from a peck on the cheek.

I stare down at Sadie, completely speechless. Happy. Encouraged by her making such a sweet gesture.

I love when she's playful and teases me, but this is a whole new ball game. And I'm up next.

I allow the giant grin that's bubbling up to take over. "Hi," I say to her, all breathily.

"Hi," she sighs back, cheeks turning a beautiful rosy pink.

"Come here." I hold out my hand, and Sadie slips hers in mine easily.

My world feels like it's righted itself with that small gesture.

I lead her out of her room and let go of her hand, placing my palm on the small of her back to guide her into the living room. Sadie makes her way to the center and slowly turns in a circle.

Her lips are parted, eyes wide as they bounce from one bouquet to another before finally settling on mine.

With a disbelieving shake of her head, Sadie whispers, "How? Why?"

I give her a shrug and explain, "You said you like peonies."

"So you got me, like what, a million of them?" Shock laces her words.

"I thought a thousand would be okay for the first time I got you flowers. We can build up to a million over the years." I hope she appreciates the little reference to the future I slipped in there.

Sadie's voice is soft with affection, lower lip trembling as an array of emotions flit across her face.

Her name is a shaky whisper across my lips. "Sadie-queen."

I take long strides over to her and enfold her in my arms. She clings to my shoulders, one hand resting on the nape of my neck.

Sadie's breath is warm against my neck as she admits, "I'm sorry, I don't mean to cry. This is just the single nicest thing anyone has ever done for me. They're lovely. You're lovely."

I loosen my grip and pull back so I can look into her eyes. I keep one arm wrapped around her as I thumb her tears away with my other hand. "You deserve so much more than this. I want you to be happy. I want to be the one who makes you happy."

"You're already doing a fantastic job." Sadie lifts onto her tiptoes and pulls me down with her grip on the back of my neck, meeting my lips with a tender kiss.

My hold on her tightens, drawing her closer as I return her kiss. Our tongues come together in a tantalizing dance, hands starting to roam, growing greedier.

"Hold on," I pant through racing breaths, my lips hovering over hers. "I have a whole date planned for us."

Unable to resist, I kiss her again. What was meant to be a press of my lips quickly turns hungry again.

I break away.

"Breakfast."

Kiss.

"Car."

Kiss.

"Date."

Kiss.

Sadie's whimper nearly undoes me, making me want to forget all the plans I made and take her straight back to her bedroom to show her the kind of loving she deserves.

She takes a step back and smiles lazily up at me. Her eyes are glassy, blissful.

Beautiful.

"Coffee first. Then breakfast. Then date." Sadie throws me the okay sign with her fingers. "I'm just going to stand in the middle of these gorgeous flowers and breathe them in before I can do anything else."

With a dazed expression, she walks to each bouquet and sticks her nose right into the blooms, inhaling deeply and letting her breath out on a contented sigh.

I think our day is off to a good start.

26

Sadie

feel like I'm floating today. It was the best start to a day I've ever had.

Coffee. Flowers. Kisses. Everett.

I don't think I need much more in life than that. And now that I've had a taste of what life could be like, it's getting harder and harder to imagine returning to my small apartment, a job I don't particularly love—or have right now—and slow living.

If Everett is serious about giving things a try, I'm going to be bold like Cece said we should be.

I'm plunging in, fully. I refuse to think about crashing down because, honestly, I feel safe with Everett. My body feels safe with him. My heart is starting to feel safe too.

That's always been the hardest thing for me to do. Fully trust with my whole heart.

I usually say I trust someone, give them ninety percent of myself, and in the end, I'm happy I reserved that final ten. When they eventually fuck me over, it hurts that little bit less.

Shoring myself up, I take a deep breath, push my shoulders back, and let my signature smirk fall into place. "So, zooms, where you taking me on this date?"

"I thought we could have lunch at my place. July is brutally hot in Vegas, and there's lots to do at night, but I want you to see the other parts of the city too, not just the Strip. The city has much more to offer than just shiny lights, no matter how enticing they are."

"I'm starting to see that." I trail my eyes down Everett's body and back up again, letting him read the clear intent behind my words.

"I'm very pleased with your keen sense of observation." He flirts right back. "Now, finish your breakfast and get ready. I'll be in my room to make a couple of calls. Come find me when you're done."

On his way past me, he bends down and places a chaste kiss on the corner of my mouth, leaving me momentarily stunned at how natural this all feels. Realizing I'm not moving, Everett gives my ass a little swat. A yelp escapes from me, a pleased moan chasing after the sound.

"Sweetheart," Everett lets out in a guttural tone. "We need to stay focused, otherwise I'm going to give you the proper spanking that you've been hankering for since we've met."

"Don't tease me if you're not going to follow through." My arousal instantly spikes at the thought of him doing just that.

"And what would you do if I did?" he challenges.

"I'd say 'thank you, sir,'" I reply in a coy tone, my eyes alight with excitement.

"Sadie-queen, don't push me. I'm currently on a razor's edge. If you don't want me to act on it, then you're going to have to run to your room. Right now."

I want Everett to lose control. I want him to take me.

Knowing how close he is to doing just that, I bend forward and wiggle my ass at him. I'm wearing nothing but a big T-shirt—having forgone my panties that are too soaked to be comfortable—now giving him a clear view of what I'm offering.

It seems to do the trick.

He snaps.

In the next second, I'm scooped up and carried to the fancy couch. Everett drops down onto it with me in his arms and gives me a fierce kiss, then flips me over, positioning me over his knee.

The anticipation of the first strike has me dripping, my breaths coming faster, tingles spreading across my skin.

"I want you to count for me, sweetheart. You're getting ten strikes. Say yes if you agree, and if it gets too much, you tell me to stop. Got it?" His words are succinct, his voice all gravel.

"Yes. Give it to me," I say in a breathy voice.

His hand lands across my bare right cheek—a sharp, delicious bite of pain, but I want more.

"One. Harder."

A second strike. Better.

"Two. More," I moan.

The third and fourth strikes follow in quick succession, my pants interrupted with cries of pleasure as my blood rushes south.

"Three. Four."

After the fifth strike, he pauses. His hand caresses my stinging flesh as words of praise fill my ears.

"Look at you, Sadie-queen. So beautiful. You have the sexiest ass I've ever seen, but with my hands making it all red, it looks even more exquisite. Like I want to take a bite out of it."

I moan at his words. They're having an even stronger effect on me than the sharp pain of his strikes. My pussy is getting wetter with each sentence, my arousal dripping down my thigh onto his black pants.

"If you like it so much, maybe you should just bite it then," I try to tease, but the words sound weak between my choppy breaths.

"Mmm... I love knowing you're enjoying this as much as I am. The decadent scent of your cunt is starting to overpower the fragrance of the peonies. I definitely know which one I prefer."

I squirm on his lap, needing some kind of friction. My pussy feels empty as I get more and more needy.

"You need something more, sweetheart? Ask for it," Everett rasps out.

Not caring how needy I sound, I beg. "Fingers. I need your fingers."

Without any preamble, Everett shoves two fingers straight into my pussy.

"Fuuuuck," he groans. "Your pussy is so tight, Sadie-queen. Look at you taking my fingers, sensational red ass on display. Listen to how wet you are for me. Is it all for me, sweetheart?"

The squelching sounds of Everett's fingers moving in and out are almost enough to embarrass me, but I can only focus on how they feel inside me.

"Yes, all for you. You make me so wet," I admit wantonly.

Everett unerringly finds my G-spot and starts massaging it, eliciting more whimpers from me.

When my pussy starts to tighten around his fingers, he languidly removes them and goes back to spanking me, wet fingers adding an extra sensation to my hot skin.

"What number was that, sweetheart? I didn't hear you count. Should I start from the beginning?" Everett asks, a hint of amusement coating his gruff tone.

"Six!"

The final four come quickly, both of us breathing hard and fast.

"Sadie-queen, I-I—" Everett's hands caress my stinging cheeks reverently as I squirm again.

I was so close.

"My fangs—they're back—" he sputters.

Knowing what's happening, I don't want him to rush out again. I want Everett to be himself with me. And if that means embracing his vampiric traits, then I want to help him any way I can.

"Bite me," I say simply.

"What? I can't." Everett refuses.

"I trust you. Where do you want to bite?"

"Your ass is all red, the blood right beneath the surface. It's like it's calling to me," Everett chokes out his admission.

"Bite me, Everett." I encourage him.

I want him to take what he needs.

The next moment, I feel twin sharp stings on my left cheek as Everett bends down and bites me. He repositions his hand and enters my pussy with his fingers.

Thumb strumming my clit, fingers massaging my G-spot, fangs sunk into my ass, and I explode.

I cry out as my orgasm takes over. My back arches in pleasure, my pussy constricts around his fingers, my nails dig into his thigh as my blood turns hot.

Limp and gasping for breath, I become aware of Everett easing his fingers—and fangs—from my body. He gently lifts me and turns me in his arms, cradling me to his heaving chest.

We cling to each other in comfortable silence as our heartbeats slowly return to normal. Everett combs his fingers through my long strands in a soothing manner.

"That was..." I start.

"Yeah. It was..." he says in quiet amazement.

"Can I see your fangs?" I ask hesitantly, lifting my head from his chest so I can look at him.

Everett grimaces and opens his mouth a fraction, baring his teeth for me.

"They're hot," I state bluntly, squirming slightly on his lap.

Everett's green eyes smolder. "Yeah?"

Studying him, I ask, "Are you okay? You're not very wordy right now."

"I'm freaking out a bit. Did I hurt you?" he asks sincerely, searching my face.

"Only in a fun way. I loved every minute. Including the bite." I wiggle my eyebrows at him.

"Good, because it might happen again. I mean, I don't have

to bite your ass again, but there's just something about your blood."

"What does it taste like?" I'm curious to know why it's happening now, all of a sudden.

"Fucking perfection. But you have to know, I've never been turned on by blood. It's one of my shortcomings as a dhampir. It's set me apart from vampires my entire life. But you, my sweet, sweet Sadie-queen, your blood sings to my soul. I crave you like nothing I've ever craved before. And I'm not so sure if it's just your blood or if it's you," he confesses earnestly.

"Well, that's a confidence booster if I've ever heard one." I try to joke. Shifting so I can frame his face with my hands, I add in a sober tone, "You can drink from me, Everett."

"I hope it doesn't come to that, but if it does, I want you to know that I've studied human anatomy at school. I was in class with the vampires and was tested on all blood-related subjects. I know where all your veins lie. I know how much I can drink at a time. I know how to keep you safe. Can you trust me with that?" Everett explains, shrewd eyes focusing intently on mine.

I place a hand on his cheek. "I can trust you with anything."

His next words die on his tongue as he analyzes my face and weighs my expression against what I just said.

"I don't deserve you," he finally utters and presses a firm kiss to my lips. "Now, let's get you sorted and fed—finally—so we can have this date."

"What about you? You've gotten me off twice already. I'm sure you're close to getting blue balls right about now."

"Sweetheart, I haven't come since I've met you. I've been denying myself until I can finally get my cock in your warm, wet cunt and can paint it with all the cum I've been saving."

And just like that, my pussy is flooded again, my heart beating at a thousand miles an hour.

"I love a good painting. I'd be your canvas any day," I say cheerfully and bounce up from Everett's lap.

My attempt at sashaying away is hindered by my stinging

ass, turning it into more of a shamble away. I glance back to see if he's watching me, guessing right, as I find his eyes fixed on my butt and his hands adjusting his aching cock.

Our day started a bit unexpectedly, but I'm definitely not complaining. I loved Sadie's reaction to the flowers I had delivered. A thousand might have been a little too much, but I have no regrets. The way her face lit up will feed my soul for years to come.

It's early afternoon when Sadie comes out of her room in black jeans and a shimmery silver top that's hanging on by a thin string around her neck, a loopy chain loosely connecting it in the back.

I thank the fates that we've crossed the physical boundaries between us because I can't wait to run my hands over the soft skin of her back. Maybe sneak my hand around under the front and toy with her nipples, and—

No. I'm going to focus.

Car. Date. House. This is the mantra I'll be repeating in my head all day.

"Sparkles, do you know how tempting you look? I'm not going to share the dirty thoughts I had just now because we'd never leave the room if I start thinking about them again. And I'm focused on wooing you today."

I grab the box I had delivered earlier and place it under my arm. With my other hand, I reach for Sadie's, lifting it to my mouth and placing a chivalrous kiss to her knuckles.

"Ms. Everly, your car awaits." I try my best impression of an English gentleman.

"Why, Mr. Ülavere, I'm charmed." She plays along, but her accent comes out more Southern than English.

I steer us toward the elevator with anticipation for the day biting at my heels.

When we get into the elevator, I draw her in front of me, tucking her back to my front and wrapping my free arm across her shoulders. She fits against me like the fates designed our bodies for each other.

Sadie leans her head back against my shoulder and holds on to my arm with both hands, snuggling closer as the elevator whirrs with its descent.

When we reach the bottom, I almost don't want to get out. But then I remember my mantra. I grab her hand and lead her to my car that's waiting for us.

With a nod to Pierce, I pass him the box and open Sadie's door for her. After she lowers herself into the seat, I lean over to buckle her in.

Sadie chuckles. "You know I can do that myself, right?"

"Just because you *can* do it doesn't mean you have to do it. Besides, I like taking care of you."

I give her a quick kiss, grab the box again, and pop it in the trunk. When I get into the driver's seat, Sadie eyes me suspiciously.

"What's with the box?"

"What box?" I ask, feigning ignorance.

"Don't play coy with me, dhampir." Sadie's so cute, narrowing her eyes and pointing a playfully accusing finger at me.

"You'll find out soon." I smile, imagining Sadie's reaction when she sees what's inside. I put a lot of thought into the gift and how I want to present it to her.

As we drive through the city, I point out various

landmarks and places that might be of interest to her. My hand rests comfortably on Sadie's thigh the entire way, her fingers tracing idle patterns on the back of my hand.

I don't know why I'm nervous, but my palms get clammy and my heartbeat becomes a solid *thump, thump, thump* in my chest the closer we get.

After parking in front of the house, I run around to get her door, grateful that she's getting used to this habit.

She gives me her hand distractedly, her eyes taking in every detail of the monolithic structure as I grab the box from the trunk.

I try to see my home from her perspective.

The two-story modern concrete structure looks slightly masculine with its clean lines and sharp corners. Its many windows allow light to flood the whole house, but the black-and-white color scheme makes it look cold against the warm desert hues.

"Let's go inside."

I tug her along and through the front door.

"That's the swimming pool, patio, outdoor dining"—I point to the left—"one bathroom and my office that way"—I point to the right—"kitchen, formal dining room, and living room straight ahead."

"Wow. You're... This is... I'm... Wow." She stumbles through her words, eyes blinking furiously as they jump around.

"Sorry if this is too much or not what you expected. Can I show you upstairs?"

Sadie nods blankly as I take her bag and drop it on a table with my cell phone. Lacing our fingers, she allows me to lead her to the main bedroom, which has an unobstructed view all the way to the Strip. It's not that visible in the daytime, but once the sun starts setting, it's clear to see.

"Wow. I wish I could give words to everything I'm feeling, seeing. I guess... spectacular. Yeah, that's it. This is spectacular." Sadie stands in front of the bed and gazes toward Vegas in the distance.

Her outfit choice blends perfectly into the monochrome bedroom. It would almost seem intentional if she had seen pictures of the place, which I know is impossible since I don't have any uploaded anywhere.

I gesture to the balcony that juts out from the large dressing room to the left. "I thought we could have dinner out here later once the temperature starts cooling a bit. Watching the Strip light up at sunset is quite a spellbinding sight."

Sadie turns her gaze to me for a second and gives me a dazzling smile. "That sounds perfect."

When Sadie's focus returns to the desert view stretching out in front of us, I slip away to the walk-in closet and place the box on the glass top of the closet island.

I zoom back to the bedroom, scared she would notice I was gone, only to find her standing in the exact same spot, with a glazed look in her eyes and a wistful smile in place.

I knew I wanted her before, but this settles something in my chest.

"Can we play rapid-fire questions again?" I interrupt her daydreaming.

"Yup. I'll go first."

"Only fair, but let's make the questions harder this time." I want to seize every moment of this date with her to get to know her on a deeper level. To dig deep into her psyche and open myself up to her probing questions too.

"Why don't you want me to meet your dad?" The question comes immediately.

It's obviously been on her mind and has bothered her ever since I said it. She deserves an honest answer, even if it's uncomfortable to talk about.

"My father is a very old vampire, like around four hundred years old. We're not close, so I'm not too sure about his actual age, nor do I care. He's from old vampire stock in Eastern Europe.

"When the Strip started building casinos, it intrigued him

and his close friends because they get horribly burned in sunlight. Vegas is very nocturnal and provides a great cover for them."

Sadie's unwavering attention is fixed on me as I speak, her head cocked to the side as she listens and nods along, seemingly taking in every word I'm saying.

I continue, "He met my human mother at a party when he was on a trip back to Eastern Europe, she was Estonian. My father apparently took some weird tonic he thought would make the night more 'exhilarating.'" I cringe just thinking about it. "Turns out his usually nonexistent vampiric sperm was exhilarated too."

I give Sadie a bland smile as I pause and take a breath. Always great to think about what a mistake I was to him and how I shouldn't even exist.

Sadie reaches forward, taking my hand in a gesture of comfort, her thumb moving reassuringly across my knuckles.

"It was only meant to be a one-night stand, but she miraculously got pregnant that night and died shortly after I was born due to birth complications. Since my existence is so rare, he came to collect me in the hopes that I had vampiric traits, but I've been a disappointment to him with my mostly human nature."

My lips turn down in a frown, and I shake my head, recalling all the demeaning insults he's spewed at me over the years. I've chosen to take the high road, to be kind to those around me, loyal, and get back at him by making a success of myself.

Taking a shuddering inhale, I go on. "I was raised by nannies and drivers and sent to Alberad as early as they allowed entry to the school. Which is around ten. Spent many vacations at friends' houses around the world instead of coming back to Vegas. Only returning if he had summoned me to bemoan my grades or curse me for something else I'd not done well enough.

"He looks down on any and all humans, no matter their status or wealth. As a fuck you to him, I changed my name as soon as I was of legal age. Then I moved to Vegas and opened my own hotel, and it's currently doing better than his. He's not been very amused by all of this."

Sadie smiles, taking obvious joy in me besting my father, but she remains silent so I can say everything I want to.

"Now, to get to your question. I can't let you meet him because you are too precious to me. He finds fault with everything I am, everything I do, but that's my burden to bear. I do not want you to be hurt by whatever he would most likely throw at you," I explain, clarifying the comment about meeting my father I made in the elevator last night, the one I'm sure made her flinch and her eyes fill with unspoken hurt.

"He sounds like a horrible male."

"He is. I really don't want you to cross paths or for you to come in contact with his snobbish ways."

Sadie's eyes widen in realization. "You were trying to protect me."

"Since the first moment I saw your electric-blue eyes," I admit, reaching forward and gently brushing one of the shorter strands of light blonde hair out of Sadie's face.

Her grip on my hand tightens as she admits in her straightforward way, "I want to kiss you. But if we start now, then we're not leaving until your cum is dripping out of me. Let's keep asking our questions before we get distracted."

I take a deep breath in and marvel at how beautifully crass she is. "Your wicked tongue is very enticing. But you make a good point. My turn. If you could have any job, what would it be?"

"Also hitting me with a serious one, I see." She's not shying away from the question, but she does bring us back from the precipice of lust we were about to tumble into.

"Seemed fair. But remember, you can veto it," I remind her.

"It's okay, it's just hard to admit out loud what's been a pipe dream that I have no way of realizing."

I tilt my head in a clear sign of listening, giving her my full attention. This time, it's me trailing a comforting touch across her knuckles.

"Something that's been a secret dream of mine would be to open a clothing boutique. Only, it would be centered around fun, flirty, sparkly clothes. And I want to make it available for renting. The average woman doesn't have enough opportunities to dress up in her daily life, and if the occasion does arrive, she doesn't have the budget to afford a whole new outfit for a onetime wear.

"It was something I thought about when I came to Vegas too. The clothes I brought will only last so long, and I want more options. But my... um... kind of unemployed state"—Sadie hesitates to say, wincing—"makes it difficult to commit to shopping.

"Anyway, my dream place would have clothes and shoes available in a range of sizes that will fit women with smaller frames to fuller ones. All-inclusive. Maybe that doesn't make it a 'smart' plan, but we're talking about dreams, right?"

I take her other hand in my free one and squeeze both. "I think that's brilliant. It would work so well in Vegas. People flying in for weekends, weddings, live shows, they all like to dress up, and if they're already paying for flights and accommodation, it only makes sense to save money where they can. Maybe the hotel could even advertise your store and it could form a package deal for bachelorette parties," I muse, thoroughly impressed with her ingenious ideas, already running through possible scenarios where I could promote her store.

"You think the idea has merit?" Sadie asks, wide eyed, seemingly astonished that I like her idea and can see a practical application for it.

"You're a smart woman. Makes you even sexier to know your brains match your beauty," I purr.

Sadie bats her eyelashes at me. "What can I say, I'm the whole package."

"You most certainly are," I admit, raising my eyebrows suggestively at her.

Getting myself back into the moment, I let go of her hands and take a step back so I can focus on our get-to-know-you game again. "Your turn to ask a question."

"Do you like living in Vegas?" she asks, one hand fiddling with the bottom of her shimmery top like it doesn't know what to do if it's not touching me.

"Oof." I clutch my heart in mock pain. She's very perceptive. "I like it well enough. I work a lot, go to the gym, meet with friends, attend some events, but it all feels a little superficial. I guess that's part of the Vegas charm. If I want to really relax, I usually travel to one of my Alberad friends' places. I'm privileged in that they're scattered around the world, so I get a change of scenery every time I visit someone.

"I do feel like there's something missing, though, something that will make me feel like I'm finally living the life I want. And I think I've found it. I've found *her*. I just need to figure out a way to hold on to her and make her want to stay."

I see the moment she catches my meaning, her heart rate picking up, her eyes going round, her jaw slack.

Before she can say anything, I swallow around the lump in my throat and casually remark, "It's my turn, isn't it?"

She nods silently, flummoxed expression still in place.

"If you were given the opportunity, would you consider staying in Vegas?" I try not to let the hopefulness seep into my voice, but I think she can detect it.

I'm a goner for her. I know it doesn't make sense, it's too fast, but nothing has felt as natural, as easy, as good, as it does with her.

"Everett." My name is a broken whisper from her mouth. "It's too fast. We've only known each other for days," she confirms what I know makes me sound crazy.

"It's okay. I don't want you to feel pressured. Forget I said anything for now. Let's see what Bertie says, and then we can revisit this conversation at a later date."

"It's not a no. It's actually—" She cuts herself off. I can practically see the wheels turning in her head before she continues.

"I like you. And everything about you. And I like Vegas. And I want to say yes. I just can't justify it to myself quite yet. Moving to a new city for a man I've only known for a couple of days is crazy, isn't it?"

"Even if he gives you the good D?" I tease.

"I've yet to see how good his D is," she retorts, giving me a pointed look.

"Maybe I can convince you?" I step closer to her.

"It would take some serious skills to throw my female instincts to the side," she says, crossing her arms.

I take another step closer until I'm right in front of her and tilt her chin up with two fingers. "Is that a challenge?"

"Temper. Temper. I wouldn't dream of challenging you," she recites.

"Wait. Are you quoting *The Lion King*?" I shift my hand until I'm cupping her jaw.

"You started it." She pouts, the smile creeping across her lips giving away her amusement.

"Tell me, are you a fan?" I trace my thumb back and forth across her cheekbone as I stare into her clever eyes.

She tracks her hand as it climbs up my black shirt and toys with the button on my sternum. "Yup, maybe we can watch it together sometime?" Her eyes flick up to mine, and apprehension and hope war with each other in their depths.

She's making plans for the future. It's not yet the level I had wished for, but these baby steps can lead to bigger ones.

"I'd love that. It's been years since I've seen it. We had limited technology available at boarding school. We ended up watching a lot of nineties movies."

"I can't imagine all the males getting into those types of movies. Some seemed so... stoic."

"It was just the environment and the stress of the situation on the island. You'd be surprised by them if you get to know them. They're great males." I defend my friends, oddly dejected that she got that impression of them.

Maybe if things work out, we can travel around the world, and she can meet them in their home environments. I think she'd really like them. I wonder if she's ever been to Paris. Or Seoul.

"I'm sorry, you're absolutely right. I think all of us were a bit out of sorts," she concedes, reaching her hand up to give mine a squeeze.

"I know we have some more questions to ask, but can I show you something?"

"Does it have anything to do with the box you've been carrying around?"

"It might," I hedge.

She bounces on the balls of her feet a little as she says, "I'm trying to play it real cool, but my curiosity is scratching at my skin. At least you have this amazing view to distract me with." She laughs.

"It'll be sunset soon, and then you'll be thoroughly distracted," I promise.

"I can't wait. But first, tell me about this box."

28

Sadie

Everett takes my hand and leads me through the luxurious bathroom to the walk-in closet. The walk-in closet that's the size of my apartment's whole living room.

I gawk at him. "This is huge. Why is it empty? Where are your clothes?"

"I use the closet on the other side of the room. This one I've been saving for my wife."

"Wife?" I blurt out.

"I mean, partner?" He sounds unsure. "Spouse? Fiancée? Girlfriend? Lover? Whatever she would prefer to be called." He gives me a sheepish smile. "But before you overthink that, I want you to have something."

He moves to the center of the room and pushes the box on the island toward me.

It's a plain white box with no markings, and my heart starts racing in anticipation. I love surprises and gifts.

Trying to draw the moment out, I slowly lift the lid to reveal a familiar dust bag.

My brows rise and my eyes go round as my expectation grows, and my heart starts pumping blood through my body at an increasingly rapid rate. I open the bag and reach in without looking, hands wrapping around rough texture and down to a sharp point. I swallow hard as my hands trace a shape I recognize from countless hours of staring at on a screen. I pull one out, then the other.

Then, my heart just about stops.

My eyes flood with tears as I stare at the most elegant pair of shoes I've ever seen.

"You got me the *Saeda 100* glitter pumps in candy pink," I whisper, my chin quivering.

With a delicate touch, I trace the crystal anklet and the dainty charm fastened to it. The glittery pump speaks to my sparkly soul.

"They're so beautiful," I remark in wonder.

"*You're* so beautiful," Everett says in a quiet voice filled with affection. "I wanted to get you something that was very *you*. I thought—and maybe it's a bit presumptuous of me—that if you consider staying, then these would look really pretty in this closet. They're yours regardless of your decision," he quickly tacks on, nerves making him rush out the last sentence.

Everett reaches out and gently tucks some blonde strands behind my ear. Then he fixes his sincere jade-green eyes on mine and, in a calm tone, says, "I just want you to know that I see you. I see what you like and what makes you happy. And if it means my shoe knowledge is now more extensive than I ever thought it could be, then I'm good with that. Do you like them?"

This male. No one has ever treated me as well as he does. Never gone out of their way, devoted time and effort to find something that's so... me.

He cares. About *me*.

I think it's time for me to admit how much I care about him too. To him, as well as myself.

"Excellent choice, I love them. Your newly acquired shoe knowledge is very impressive." I try to joke, but my voice is wobbly with emotion.

"Do you want to try them on?"

"Not right now."

Everett looks taken aback by my statement, hurt marring his features.

Before he can get too discouraged, I add, "I want to fuck you."

His eyes light up, and his frown turns into a smirk. "Do you, now?"

"But first, kiss me, so I can show you how much I like these shoes, how much I like *you*."

Everett surges forward and slants his mouth over mine, reaching his warm hands around me, smoothing over the bare skin of my back. Our tongues meet in a hot, slick kiss, turning hungrier with each stroke of our tongues.

With one hand, I clasp the back of his head and pull him closer, tracing down the buttons of his shirt with the other.

I break our kiss to mutter demandingly against his lips, "Off," as I fail to undo a button, my hands fumbling with my strengthening craving for more of this male.

He leans back and grips the collar of his shirt, the veins on the backs of his hands and his forearms standing out more severely as his arms flex, and he rips the shirt down the middle, buttons popping off as the material parts.

"Holy shit. That was hot," I breathe out, my voice thick with desire.

It's the sexiest thing I've seen in my life.

My hands hover, attempting to help, but I'm stunned at the sight of his defined chest and rippling abs. My tongue darts out to wet my lips, and I swallow. It's the first time I've given his abs a proper look.

"Like what you see, sweetheart?" The smugness in Everett's voice is diminished by his own hunger.

"Maybe." My own sarcasm is not as effective as I swallow down the extra saliva that has gathered in my mouth.

Of their own accord, my fingers start mapping the valleys

between each muscle, down from his pecs—lower—between each ab—lower—until reaching the delicious V of his hips as he stands stock-still, letting me explore his body.

I drag my fingers along the stark lines, working from the outside in, and reach for the button of his pants, flick it open, and pull the zipper down.

My gaze turns wanton as I peer up at him with hooded lids and slowly sink to my knees in front of him, fingers hooked in his waistband, tugging his pants and underwear down with me. He steps out of them, and I unceremoniously chuck them into a corner.

"Sadie-queen..." My name is a prayer on Everett's lips as his long, stiff cock bobs in front of me.

I'm hungry for him. I want to taste him. Consume him. Make him mine.

The thoughts come completely unbidden and catch me off guard for only a second, until I sink into their truth and acknowledge the depth of my emotions.

I'm all in.

With my mind set, I smile up at Everett, and in the coyest tone I can muster, I ask, "Can I suck your cock now, zooms?"

"Fuck, sweetheart. You never have to—"

I cut him off with the swipe of my tongue over the head of his cock, licking up the bead of precum that was beckoning me.

With a breathy moan, I confess, "You taste so good."

My pussy is getting slick from that one taste of him.

Everett's green eyes turn black, and his fangs descend. The air grows even thicker with our lust, our need for each other amplifying with every beat of our hearts.

I try to wrap my fingers around his cock, but he's too thick, and I thank whatever power put this male in my life.

He's going to ruin me with that anaconda in the best way.

I give his cock a small tug, and Everett's head falls back as a beastly rumble claws up from deep in his chest. The sound is so primal that it makes my pussy gush.

"Sadie-queen..." is all he manages.

Moving my mouth to the twin of my tattoo on his thigh, I give it a chaste kiss before shifting and licking a straight line up from the base of his cock to the tip.

The hitch of Everett's breath is like music to the deepest part of my soul. It makes me feel powerful. This gorgeous, strong male, giving me the reins to his body, makes me that much more confident in my decision to stay.

Eager hands shoot forward to my hair, his touch gentle as he smooths the strands out of my face and loosely gathers it into a ponytail, giving him an unobstructed view of what I'm about to do to him.

"Better hold on," I say right before guiding him into my mouth and sucking.

I bob up and down, twist my hand around the base of his cock, and luxuriate in the sounds of Everett's breathing rapidly growing more labored as he tries to keep from thrusting.

I alternate licking and sucking and test out methods to make him gasp, scraping my teeth along his length, taking him deep to hit the back of my throat, deeper. His legs are vibrating with the need to move, but he's holding absolutely still, letting me take him how I want to.

My panties are soaked. I know the scent of my arousal must be seeping into the walls with how turned on I am from bringing him pleasure, and I bask in the feeling that this all could be mine.

That this *is* mine.

Taking a deep breath, I relax my throat and swallow him down as far as my throat can allow his thick length.

"Sweetheart, no, I don't want to hurt you." Everett eases his cock from my mouth. "I'm too big. I'd rather take care of you. Why are you still clothed?" he admonishes, his breathing still too rapid to sound stern.

"Don't you want to fuck my throat, zooms?" I play pout, my voice husky with need.

"I'd rather fuck your delicious cunt, sweetheart."

Without delay, I reach behind me and undo the clasps holding my top in place, tossing it to the corner with his clothes.

In front of me, Everett's knees hit the floor, and his hands gravitate to my breasts, cupping, weighing, massaging them.

"These tits are perfect. Look at these rosy nipples, they're begging me to taste them, aren't they?"

Everett's mouth finds a nipple, and he carefully sucks on it, then lightly scrapes a fang over it. The sensation sends a shudder through me and I whimper. He laves the sting with a swirl of his tongue, then repeats the motion on the other side.

I become a sobbing mess—whines, moans, mewls falling from my lips—the pleasant warmth of his mouth a delicious contrast to the scrapes of pain. My grip on Everett's shoulders, his head, is strong, clawing, wanting more.

I push at his shoulder, and he moves back willingly, confusion and intrigue etching his face.

"I'm going to fuck you now," I pant, nearly feral with need. A need for this male, a need to connect our most carnal beings. "Lie back."

"I can't fuck you on the closet floor the first time. I need to woo you with flowers and bedrooms—romance," Everett protests weakly, lowering himself down.

"You've done the flowers already. Good job with that. Let's use the bed next time. I just need *your* cock in *my* pussy, right now, right here," I say imploringly, unbuttoning my pants.

I let him look his fill as I peel my pants off as elegantly as jeans with a damp crotch allow to be taken off. He sweeps his eyes over my body appreciatively with a rumbly "hmmm" coming from deep in his chest, bolstering my confidence.

I climb on top of him, straddling his thighs, his thick cock bobbing in front of my pussy, as if searching for my heat, his hands coming to rest on my legs.

"Are you ready for me?" I purr.

"Very. Condom?" Everett rasps.

"IUD and recently tested."

"No one since my last tests."

Not needing any more assurance, I shift forward and guide his cock to my pussy. His head nudges at my opening, and we both groan as I sink down, inch by delicious inch.

My thighs start to tremble as I brace myself on his chest, slowly trying to take all of him, but he's just so big.

"Sweetheart, look at you taking my big cock in your tight little cunt like the queen that you are," Everett chokes out his praise, voice ragged, chest heaving, hands smoothing up and down my thighs.

"You're... so... big. Can't... fit," I stammer out, eyes closed as I give my pussy a moment to adjust, hovering with half his cock inside me.

"It'll fit," Everett declares confidently. "Let me take over, sweetheart. Let me fuck you like you need to be fucked."

I open my eyes and make sure to look deep into his darkened gaze, ensuring he sees the weight of my next words. "Fuck me like I'm yours."

Everett blinks. He processes the meaning for a moment, then I'm scooped up and carried to the bedroom, dick still half inside me.

Affectionate hands lower us onto the bed as one. My back hits the mattress, and he bends me until my knees are kissing my ears, eyes lasered on where we're joined.

"So tight. So slick. So warm," Everett grits out.

"Good. More. Cock. Now," I pant.

He smirks down at me and thrusts himself to the hilt. My lusty moan at being filled so completely is met with an equally satisfied groan from him.

Staying preternaturally still, he gives me a moment to adjust until I'm squirming for more. Our breaths harsh, sharp. Hearts beating wildly.

I reach for his face and frame it in my hands, ready to be brave and utter something aloud that'll change the course of my life, something I've only admitted to myself mere moments ago.

"I choose you, Everett. I choose Vegas. I'm staying, if you want me to."

His eyes blaze with delight, his fangs peeking out from his brilliant smile. "I'm yours, and now I'm going to fuck you like you're mine. Hold on."

That's all the warning I get until he starts thrusting into me like he's trying to brand me with his cock. The wet sounds of my pussy accompanied by my panting mewls encourage him for more, harder, faster.

Everett shifts us once again so he's sitting, leaning back on his haunches, arms banded around me. He positions me to straddle him across his thighs, legs wrapped around his waist.

I claw at his shoulders as I bounce up and down on his cock, and he thrusts up into me from below. The new angle provides the perfect stimulation for my clit.

Our bodies form their own orchestra with the sound of slapping skin, breaths sawing in and out, his rugged groans of exertion, and my intensifying cries of pleasure.

"Sadie-queen, I need you to come. Can you do that for me, sweetheart?" Everett rasps.

"Close, I'm so close," I sob.

"What do you need?"

"Bite me."

"What?" His hips almost falter, but at my whimper, he resumes his rhythm.

"Bite me, zooms." I tilt my head and bare my throat to him, inviting him to sink his teeth into me.

"Are you—"

Before he can finish that sentence, I shove his head down into my neck. Everett's fangs pierce my skin and sink into the exact spot he needs to feed from.

The bite of pain sends me careening over the edge.

"Everett!"

I clasp his head tighter as he sucks on my neck, my hips grinding down, a tremor working its way up my spine as I come.

My pussy pulses around his cock, and he thrusts into me once, twice, and then he's coming too. Warm cum shoots into me, painting my pussy as he promised he would.

Everett slowly retracts his fangs from my throat, lapping at the wounds, causing goose bumps to barrel down my limbs. I thought it would hurt, but it was the perfect balance of pleasure and pain.

With his cock still in me, eyes closed, chest rising and falling with the rapid breaths of his climax, Everett asks, "So, the D is good enough to stay?"

"It totally is," I sigh and squeeze my core muscles around him.

29

Everett

My life will never be the same again. Sex with Sadie was unlike anything I've ever experienced before. The way she commanded my body, commanded me, was so hot. But the most remarkable thing was the way she gave herself to me.

I feel like something has shifted in my body, my mind, and my heart.

I prop myself up on my side, resting my head on my hand as I admire a sated Sadie next to me in my bed. The moonlight casts her pale skin in a silver glow, reflecting off her light blonde hair splayed across the pillow.

"Sadie-queen," I whisper, brushing the silky hair out of her face.

She looks like a goddess, body naked, limbs tangled in white sheets.

Sadie opens one eye and gives me a lazy smile. "Ready for round two?" she drawls.

"Not quite yet," I chuckle. "Well... actually, yeah," I confirm, giving my stiff cock a tug, imagining Sadie's wet heat wrapped around it. "I want to ask you something first, though."

At the gravity in my tone, she pushes up on her elbows and gives me an inquisitive look, so I go on. "Do you feel anything different in your body? Like maybe your chest area?"

"I'm assuming you're not talking about the fang scrapes on my tits?" Sadie asks, completely serious, looking down at her bare chest.

"No, I'm thinking more along the lines of the tug we would feel when we were far away from each other."

"Hold on, let me feel it out." Sadie closes her eyes, brows scrunched up in concentration, the rapid movement under her eyelids evidence of her search.

Eyes popping open, her electric-blue gaze stares up at me. "It's you. I think," she surmises, voice rich with wonder.

"I think so. It's like I can sense you too. Right in my chest, my heart. Does it feel like that to you too?"

"Yeah, that's exactly it. What does it even mean?"

"I think it's time we give Bertie another call and see if this helps his research. But first, I want to try something."

"Sure. What do you have in mind?"

"I'm curious if the shift has anything to do with our connection, our distance limit. I'm wondering if the hundred-yard rule is still in place," I muse.

"Want to try it out? Let me get dressed, and then we can test it."

Sadie's easy trust in me warms my body from the inside out.

She gets out of the bed and walks to her closet, her nude body splendid in the pale moonlight coming through the windows. I'm feeling awfully happy that the glass is one-way and that I don't have to worry about neighbors spying on her beautiful body, but just to be sure, I keep the lights off.

In my head, I had a whole day planned. Watch the sunset, see the Strip light up in the distance, dinner, then maybe things would naturally progress. But I'm finding that life is very unpredictable with Sadie, in the best way possible.

When she struts back into the bedroom, she's still naked,

holding her clothes in her hand. Naked, except for her new glittery shoes on her feet.

"They fit like a glove. How did you know my size?" Sadie says, standing in front of the mirror and assessing her shoes from all angles.

"I may have done some snooping," I admit with something between a wince and a shrug, not quite sure if I should be proud of my sleuthing skills.

"Weirdly, I don't mind. Thank you." Sadie walks to the bed and places a knee on the mattress. Cupping my jaw, she gives me a wet kiss. Right as the kiss is about to turn ravenous, she leans away. "Can I borrow a shirt? My jeans are kind of... damp."

The mental image of her in my clothes, with those shoes, and the just-fucked hair she's currently sporting, has all my blood pumping straight to my cock.

I take a deep breath with the hope of centering myself, but the air is rife with the smell of sex and Sadie's arousal. I want my house to smell like this, always.

Before I allow myself to do my cock's bidding, I take Sadie's hand and walk to my closet. I turn on the lights, dimming them to their lowest setting, and pull on some sweats. I find my favorite button-down for Sadie as she skims her fingers along the other shirts.

"You really like black, don't you?" Sadie teases.

"Some of them are charcoal, raven, ebony, obsidian..." I justify. "But this one is the most comfortable."

I hold it out for her as she threads her arms through before I fasten the buttons. The moment feels very domestic, very right, and I smile to myself.

"What's that smile for, zooms?" Sadie asks, tone kind and curious.

"Just how right it feels to have you here like this," I reply, not quite meeting her eyes, afraid what she said earlier was only in the heat of the moment.

Sadie reaches forward and grips my chin between two fingers, lowering my face until my eyes are locked on hers. "I meant what I said. I want to stay. Nothing has ever felt this natural. This real," she confesses fiercely. Her grip loosens, hand moving to her own heart. In a smaller voice, she adds, "I don't want to sabotage my own happiness by being scared. I'm giving you one hundred percent of my heart. Please keep it safe."

Needing to reassure her, I cup Sadie's face with both my hands, her hands resting on my waist, as we stare deeply into each other's eyes, baring our deepest selves to one another.

"Sadie, you're the most beautiful creature I've ever laid eyes on. And not just your physical body. Your soul calls to mine. I want to know you more and more each day. The fates might have pushed us together or orchestrated our meet-cute, but right here, right now, I'm choosing *you*. I want *you*."

Right along with that confession, it feels like a veil is lifted from my eyes.

Puzzle pieces are slowly slotting into place in my head. I'm starting to understand the events that took place on the island, over the last few days, things about myself, but mainly...

Sadie.

Sadie at the center of it all.

At the center of me.

"We choose each other," she says affectionately, eyes gleaming with emotion, a pink blush whispering across her cheeks.

"We do." My lips find hers, sealing an unspoken promise between us.

"Is that—Did you—I mean, this is going to sound so weird. This desire." She rubs at her chest. "Is that your emotion I'm feeling?"

"I believe it is. I can feel a bit of yours too."

"How does that even work?"

"This is what I need to confirm with Bertie. My theory is that the bond between us has evolved. Once we made an intentional commitment to each other, even before saying the words aloud, it strengthened. This happens in some species, but I've never heard of it in relation to dhampirs or vampires. Remember Rollo? He's a wolf shifter, and it's very common in his species. It's a sacred bond, deeper than marriage." I wince. "Hope that doesn't freak you out now."

"It's oddly comforting. And I guess I feel... special."

"Not to sound like a broken record, but you are."

"Har, har. Let's go try this bond thing out, see if that limit is still in place."

"You saying you need some distance from me?"

"I have an idea of something I'd like to do—privately. It would be so much easier to plan if I've got a bit of distance from you."

"Now I'm really intrigued."

"Not happening. Put on a shirt, zooms. And let's see if you can make it more than a hundred yards from me."

Deciding not to push her any more on that topic for now, I do as she says and grab the closest T-shirt.

"I think your phone is still downstairs," I say as I thread my fingers through hers and lead her toward the stairs. "We can use them like last time. If you get a tug, then let me know, and I'll come rushing back."

"Sure. Am I still saved as 'sparkly princess' on your phone?" Sadie asks when we reach the living room.

"Nope." I pick up my phone from the table and turn it so she can see for herself.

"You saved me as 'Sadie Queen'? When?"

"The first night I kissed you. You were never meant to be a princess, always a queen. And I hope to treat you as such, every day," I admit, an unexpected flush working its way to my cheeks, making my ears burn.

"Want to see what your name is saved as in my phone?" Sadie asks, picking up her phone and holding it to her chest.

"Honestly, I'm too scared to ask."

Sadie turns her phone and shows me the screen.

My burst of laughter startles me.

King Cock.

Sadie's giggles join me, her eyes filling with tears. "Looks like we really are meant to be together. A king and queen. I think we can say we both won in our little wager," she stutters through her laughter.

Once we calm down enough, I plant an appreciative kiss on her lips and tap her ass on my way out the door.

I run down the dark street, enjoying the balmy summer evening—a reprieve from the scorching desert heat in the daytime. Getting close to the distance limit, I call her phone.

"You ready, sparkles? I'm almost there."

"Did I get demoted back to sparkles now?"

"I think I like having a list of nicknames that I can swap out, depending on how well you behave."

"Ah, I see. So, what do I get called if I'm being naughty?" Her voice has gone husky, a near purr coming across the line.

I can imagine her twirling a strand of hair around her finger with her head cocked just so...

"Anything I want, as long as you know that you'll get another spanking."

"Ooo, promises, promises," Sadie taunts.

"Not that I want to change the topic, but are you still okay? No tugs?"

"I'm good, but I can sense your amusement. And horniness. Are you walking out there with a hard-on?"

"I've been sporting a semi since we met. Was starting to get some serious blue balls before today."

"We can't have that now, can we? How far away are you?"

"Why? You want to do something about it?"

"I have a couple of things in mind. I think I'll head up to the shower, I'm still sticky with your cum. Come find me once you're back," she teases.

I've never moved as fast as the moment she says that. Satisfied that the distance limit is no longer in place, I race back from about five hundred yards away to scoop her into my arms.

The shriek that comes from Sadie when my arms band around her will forever be imprinted in my memory.

I deposit her right in front of the shower and bend to take off her shoes.

"How the fuck do these things come off? My fingers can't get the clasp," I say, fingers fumbling with the dainty strap around her ankle.

"I'll get them. Come here," Sadie says, tugging at my shirt.

She slips it off for me, and we quickly get each other undressed. She bends forward to give me a beautiful view of her naked ass, her cunt glistening with arousal, as she swiftly unclasps her shoes.

With roaming hands, we make it into the shower, hot water raining down on us from the dual rain shower heads.

Wet kisses turn hungry, hands groping, as we need more and more of each other.

"How can you taste and smell so good all the time?" I say against her open mouth, licking into it, needing more.

I trace her collarbone with wet kisses, and she tilts her neck to give me better access as her nails scratch at my back, her other hand fisting my hard cock.

Sadie swings her leg up around my hip, grinding her cunt against me.

"Want me to beg?"

"Yes, actually."

"Pretty, please. Give me your monster cock. Shove it in my pussy—"

I spin Sadie around and bend her over, shoving my cock into her tight cunt like she wanted.

My hands grip her hips hard as my thrusts turn brutal, Sadie's crescendoing moans encouraging me to be rough with her.

I shift one hand to Sadie's hair and wrap it around my fist, forcing her back to arch at the most sensual angle.

Her hands are splayed against the glass, our reflection staring back at us from the mirror against the wall on the other side of the shower.

She looks so exquisite with her face scrunched up in ecstasy, luscious lips parted with her panting breaths.

Our fucking is hard, fast.

"Open your eyes, sweetheart. Look how well you take this king cock. Told you you're a queen."

My fangs descend as my climax looms, my hand reaching around to strum Sadie's clit, my eyes riveted on the pulse jumping in her neck.

"Everett, you can bite me."

"No. I already bit you earlier. I don't want to drain you."

"You didn't take that much, right? You said you studied blood and anatomy. I trust you. Bite me." Sadie's words are strained as she fights off her release.

At her invitation, I rub harder and faster at her clit, feeling her choking my cock, her cunt getting tighter and tighter with each thrust. When her muscles start to lock up, I go in, striking my fangs into her neck.

The taste of her blood is like a balm to my soul, an aphrodisiac to my cock, triggering my own climax.

Together, we fall over the edge so beautifully. Our bodies pulsing, breaths stuttering, shouts echoing off the tiled walls, while our souls entwine around each other.

With a blissed-out smile, I ease my cock out of Sadie. She turns to face me with an equally satisfied expression, heavy-lidded eyes blinking slowly.

"You know, I had a vision of this exact scene the first night we met. So happy that it wasn't just my imagination."

"Was it this good in your dream?"

"Nothing could compare to this. To you. You fuck like a

god."

"Like a king," I correct. "Your king. Now let's wash up before my cock gets ideas for another round in the shower."

"Oh fuck no. My pussy just took a pounding, and your cum is still leaking out of me. Give me a moment to recover before you put that anaconda inside me again."

"Are you sore? I didn't detect hurt in the bond."

"No, no. You disrespected me so good back there. Five stars. Do recommend." Sadie holds up five fingers to emphasize her rating.

"I'll be sure to disrespect you regularly now," I say as I mentally make a list of ways I could bring her just as much pleasure or even more.

"Thank fuck."

I place her in the center of the shower and lather her with soap before starting on her hair.

We slowly wash each other, eventually stumbling into bed, and get sweaty all over again.

Everett and I emerge from the bedroom only around lunchtime, starving for sustenance after so many orgasms throughout the night that I lost count.

In the kitchen, Everett's hands never leave my body. Mine never leave his. We're insatiable with our touches, our kisses.

"I messaged Bertie earlier. I told him I have an update about our distance limit," Everett says around a bite of sandwich I just fed him. I'm propped on the kitchen island, Everett standing between my legs as we alternate eating and swapping kisses. "He scheduled a group call with everyone who was on the island."

"Do you think any of the others will have an update too?" I ask, nipping at the finger he's wiping my lip with.

He puts his finger in his mouth and sucks the food off it. "I think they might. Maybe some of them are like us and giving things a real go," Everett says with a soft smile and presses a kiss to my mouth.

I put down my sandwich and wrap my arms around this sweet male. I feel myself becoming more attached to him with each moment that passes, my respect and adoration for him growing stronger.

I think I'm falling for him.

"I hope so. They all deserve to feel as happy as I do right now," I say tenderly into his ear, and he pulls me closer to him. Sandwich all but forgotten.

"Sadie-queen..." His voice is thick with affection as he squeezes me tighter to him before loosening his arms to look into my watery eyes. Green gaze intent on mine, he says, "I never thought I'd find someone as special as you. Happy is an understatement for how I feel when I'm with you. I'm so excited about the future we're building together."

"Me too. Now that I'm staying, I better start on my job search." I smile at the idea of building a new future in Vegas. With Everett.

"About that"—he holds up a finger—"I have an idea. But let's start the job discussion later. We need to finish up here before Bertie calls. He's super punctual and will most probably be annoyed if we're not all online before the set time."

We eat our sandwiches quietly, still keeping our eyes locked on each other, and move to Everett's office.

It's a sleek, masculine room with dark wood furniture and a black-and-gray color palette. The rug is thick and soft on the wooden floors, muffling our steps toward his desk.

I make to grab a chair for myself, but he just drags me onto his lap as he prepares his computer. Settling into his embrace behind the desk, I breathe him in.

This moment, this house, him, it feels meant to be.

I feel home.

Before I get a chance to say anything, the call comes through.

Ten separate boxes appear like a synchronized dance, all the guys evidently attuned to Bertie's quest for punctuality.

"Good day, my brethren and your partners," Adelbert's formal voice greets us as Everett's hand splays possessively across my waist.

I wave at Cece, who is sitting next to him, keeping a

respectable distance from his touch. Clearly, they haven't had any physical contact yet.

"I am pleased to report that my search has been fruitful. Be that as it may, my findings might be met with some misgivings," he forewarns us all.

"Before I undertake the explanation, is there anyone who would like to share if their status has changed? Everett, perhaps?"

My eyes scan over the different images, recognizing all the girls from the boat, and I smile to myself. A few are looking rather cozy with their 'partners'—I wonder if we can just call them boyfriends now—and some even...

Oh, who's the other male with Natalie and Jasper? Does he know what's going on? I turn my head to whisper the question to Everett just as he starts to speak.

"Sadie and I have just discovered that our distance limit doesn't exist anymore," Everett announces proudly, nuzzling his head into me.

My smile stretches across my lips, a flush working its way up my chest, blooming high on my cheeks.

"How'd that happen?" Jamie asks, leaning forward in his chair. "Iris and I haven't tested it since the island. Not been in the mood for another broken nose."

Chuckles come from numerous screens, and a few shake their heads in amusement at the memory.

"Allow me to explain," Adelbert interrupts the laughter. "I have communicated with Everett as well as the few who have had status changes. This aligns with my findings."

"Who else had changes?" I ask quietly to Everett, whose other hand is now stroking up my bare thigh.

"That matter is private to them. If *they* would like to share it with the others present on this call, then they are free to do so. I will not compel anyone to publicly divulge sensitive or private information at this point," Adelbert answers, stern as ever.

Cece looks at him from the corner of her eye, a half smile

pulling at her lips as she gives an almost imperceptible shake of her head.

I wonder what that's about. *Message Cece after this*, I tell myself.

I turn my head and mouth to Everett, "Was that too loud?"

"Don't worry about it," Everett says in a hushed tone, lips pressed to my ear, following his words with a nibble on my earlobe.

His hand slips higher and starts tracing the tattoo on my thigh.

I bite my lip as I try to contain my whimper and focus on the conversation. My eyes, however, have a mind of their own as they jump from tiny screen to tiny screen, studying their occupants.

I cock my head and narrow my eyes when I get to Diana's square. Rollo is sitting next to her, and what looks like two carbon copies of him are standing behind their couch, hovering close by with their arms crossed over their broad chests. I wonder what's going on there...

Adelbert's voice startles me back into the moment. "Has anyone heard of a *fated* bond? Not to be mistaken with a mated bond."

Furrowed brows, tilted chins, and slow shakes of heads are his silent answers. It's clear no one has a clue what that is.

"I thought that might be the case," he continues. "A fated bond is brought on by the stars aligning to bring two, or more, people together. The fates choose the partners and orchestrate the events leading to their meeting."

Helena scoots forward in her seat and raises her hand slightly for attention. "So you're saying that us chartering the boat was not by chance but rather by fate's design? What happened to free will?"

Iris addresses her friend gently, "Lenny, that's kind of true. We followed up with the company, and that yacht doesn't exist on their books. They have other boats, but not the one we took. It doesn't make sense to me, but then again, none of this does." She shrugs.

Jamie picks up her thread. "We ambled down to the beach the morning when everyone left, and there was no evidence of your little picnic. Not even a cushion or a piece of litter."

Adelbert takes over the explanation. "It seems that the boat was sent by the fates. That they nudged you along, so to speak, all the way to the island and past all the wards."

Helena lets out a long, slow sigh. "And everyone remarked on how easy it was for us to get random women we met to join us on the cruise. We thought it was all organic. My trust issues just climbed to brand-new heights. Thanks, fates."

That gets a couple of giggles from the women, nods abounding on the screens. All the while, Everett's fingers continue their lazy pattern on my thigh.

Adelbert continues, "I'd like to expound on the bond. The fated bond causes forced proximity, but it still gives you the choice of getting to know your partner. According to the lore I found, this is a rare occurrence, only to appear about once every thousand years, depending on if the fates deem it necessary."

"Ah, Bertie, you saying we're special?" Jasper jokes, pouting his lips and batting his eyes at the screen.

I'm curious about where they're located now. All three of them in that screen are dressed in wintery sweaters.

"That's precisely what I'm saying, Jasper." Adelbert's tone is solemn as always. "Can I continue, or does anyone else have a joke to make?" He lets out an exasperated breath and runs his hand through his platinum hair.

Cece glances up at him, her eyes wide with concern. If I can pick up on that nervous tick, she surely did too.

"As I was saying, the fates orchestrate your meeting and then give you the choice of staying together. If you get to know your partner and *choose not* to pursue a romantic relationship, the bond will dissolve after a certain amount of time, the distance limit will be erased, and you can return to your life as if nothing had happened. I believe the marking will also fade at that time."

Cordelia, looking down at her wrist and then at Erik's, asks, "Why doesn't he just say tattoo?"

Pretending he didn't even hear her, Adelbert goes on, "Though, if you make physical contact with your partner, the bond will grow stronger. I believe the *urge* to be close to your partner becomes intense and perhaps even uncomfortable, so please proceed with caution."

"What if we like the touch and *'urges'*?" Jamie mimics Adelbert's tone and throws a wink at the camera.

Adelbert's deep inhale is loud, his shoulders rising with the effort to not respond to the taunting from his friends.

Cece leans toward Adelbert, her voice low with a sweetness all her own. "Don't mind them. Just keep telling us what you found."

Everett says, "Sorry, Bertie. We're listening. What does it mean if we choose to pursue a romantic relationship?"

"Thanks, Everett. If you *choose to* pursue the relationship, grow genuine feelings for each other, and make a conscious *choice* to be together, then the fated bond becomes a mate bond."

A couple of gasps come from the screen, but I can't quite make out from who. It sounded like a mix of masculine and feminine gasps.

"So we can become fated mates?" Edmond asks in wonder, his wings splaying out a bit at the question.

I wonder what that means in gargoyle body language.

"Yes. If you choose it. Fate only brings you together, but becoming mates is a choice." Adelbert looks weary, older, as he finishes his explanation. "Any questions?"

Daehan unmutes himself and asks, "How does that work for different species? Rollo, fated mates are plentiful in your species, right? Could similar traits be found in others?"

"My guess is that you'll have to research species-specific resources. I have not found sufficient time for that yet but wanted to provide you with the information I currently have available,"

Adelbert explains.

"If I may?" Everett says, his hand now cupping my pussy under the desk, fingers leisurely tracing my lips, not quite entering. I know he's aware of the state of my desire as it's dripping down my thighs and onto his pants.

Without waiting for a reply from Adelbert, Everett continues, "Sadie and I have chosen to pursue a romantic relationship. We've chosen to stay together."

Cece's head snaps up at that, and I wince. I was hoping to tell her myself, but things happened too quickly. I give her a small apologetic wave and gesture with my hands that I'll call her later. She purses her lips to keep her smile at bay, an "I told you so" dancing in her eyes as she wiggles her brows at me.

"We were the first couple to make physical contact, and our bond definitely strengthened over time. It's always been present. Our personalities, though, took the lead in our connection. Some things I noticed about my nature also came to the forefront. I've had elongated canines my whole life, but now, at certain times, I have fangs that descend. I've also never been drawn to blood, but Sadie's calls to me. And it tastes fucking extraordinary. Her scent.... Don't even get me started." Everett clears his throat and shifts in his seat. "This is just to say that some of my more *primal* urges come out with Sadie. I don't know what that would be like for each of your species. Just thought it would be good to be made aware of it," Everett adds as I squirm in his lap and grind back on his hard cock pressing against me.

The fact that he just told all his friends how much he likes me and how good my blood tastes turns me on. Now I want to reward him for this bold declaration, and I have the perfect idea for how I can achieve it.

On the inside, I have a full-blown Grinch smile stretching my face when I think of how he'll react to my plan.

Everett continues his humble boasting. "Since we made the choice to be together and, um, consummated it"—cheers

rise up at that as I watch my face turn bright red on the screen—
"both Sadie and myself have felt a bond develop in our chests. We
have a slight read on each other's emotions and a general sense of
awareness of the other. It's not intrusive or anything, I rather like it,"
he says, planting a wet smack of his lips on my cheek.

He goes on in a more sincere tone. "I have not heard of
this kind of mating bond in vampire species. I'm considering myself
lucky and thanking the fates for bringing my Sadie-queen to me
and providing me with a deep connection to her."

Everett hugs me closer to him with his arm banded around
me, a digit on his other hand slipping into my pussy and lazily
stroking in and out so as not to alert the others of what's happening.
I doubt he would want to make me orgasm in front of his friends.
I hope not.

Cece's smile is filled with pride and happiness for me, yet I
see her own hurt and longing in her eyes. She makes the same call-
you-later gesture I made earlier.

"That was certainly insightful. Thank you for sharing your
personal findings with us, Everett. If there are no other questions,
then we can wrap up this call. But to summarize: you've got a
fated bond with forced proximity, it can intensify with touch, it
can dissolve over time, or it can strengthen into a mate bond if
you choose it to be so." Adelbert recaps the bullet points of the
conversation.

Harvey nods his appreciation. "Thanks for all your hard
work and for finding answers. We will settle the matters between
ourselves and alert you to any status changes along the way." Helena
nods warily along next to him.

"Get some rest, Bertie. You look like you haven't slept in
ages. We appreciate you scheduling this call and for all the hours
you poured into the research," Everett adds, voice serious as he adds
a second finger into my opening, his thumb now rubbing slow
circles on my clit.

I try to keep a straight face as goose bumps ripple across

my skin. Everett's expression is stoic, but the wicked glint in his eye is obvious as I keep my gaze trained on his face on the screen.

"You are most welcome. Have a nice day all," Adelbert says and instantly signs off, effectively ending the call for everyone.

Everett loosens his arm around me to turn the computer off, his other hand deftly finding my G-spot and stroking it, the pressure on my clit increasing.

I pant as I start writhing against his hand, my breathing becoming more labored. A stark contrast to his calm, methodical tidying up. I would think he was unaffected if it wasn't for the hard length in his sweats pushing against me.

"What do you need, zooms?" I pant.

"I need your sweet cunt, sweetheart. Announcing to my friends that you're staying was one of my proudest moments, but it's also made me a bit feral with the need to claim you again. Think you can take me, Sadie-queen?" Everett's sweet words come out choked, voice thick with lust, making my pussy even wetter.

My clit takes on a pulse of its own as all my blood rushes to the area.

"Take me, Everett."

"Fuck, hearing you say my name..." His words come out on a growl. "I'm not going to be gentle right now. If you don't like what I'm doing just tell me to stop."

Everett stands up from his chair and pushes my chest down against the desk with his body, fingers still inside me. With his free hand, he pushes his sweats down and hikes my shirt up over my ass.

A tremor rolls down my body in anticipation as Everett positions his cock against his fingers, slowly pulling them out as he guides his cock into me, my wetness easing his way into my pussy. He pushes in deeply, seating himself fully in one smooth motion.

The two fingers covered in my arousal replace his thumb on my clit, and he moves his other hand to my throat to hold me still, perfectly at his mercy.

This time Everett doesn't wait for me before he starts

thrusting.

Being held like this, like I'm a tool for his pleasure, is the hottest sexual experience of my life. He plays my body like it's an instrument he's mastered. He's taking, taking, taking from me. I'm loving it so much that soon I'm screaming his name, convulsing around his cock.

Everett doesn't slow his thrusts. He fucks into me like he has a point to prove, to me, to the world—I don't care who, I'm just along for the ride.

His breathing turns harsh as I repeatedly cry out his name, chanting it. His grip on my throat grows tighter, not quite restricting my airway, but the threat is there. Everett starts rubbing my clit harder and faster as his cock starts to thicken in me, signaling how close he is.

"Come for me again, Sadie-queen." He releases my throat and nips at my neck with his fangs, not quite breaking skin, and I come undone.

We explode together, sensations racing through my body, my core clamping tight around his cock as he spills into me.

He keeps his cock in me as he lowers us back into his desk chair, our chests moving up and down in synchronized breaths. I go limp on him, my body overwhelmed with the pleasure he's wrung from me.

"You good?" Everett says into my hair, arms draped loosely around my body.

"A girl can get used to days like this," I sigh into him.
"I hope so," is his response as he places a kiss on my neck.

Sadie: Sorry I didn't tell you sooner. Things happened quite fast. I'm staying in Vegas!

Cece: Haha *laughing emoji* I thought you might. You two are perfect for each other *heart eyes emoji*

Sadie: We'll need to figure out visiting dates. I'd love to come see the forest. And you *face blowing a kiss emoji*

Cece: I'd love to see you too! Let's do a video chat soon. I want to hear all about how he convinced you to stay.

Sadie: I'm embarrassed to say it wasn't too difficult. But some pretty shoes might have helped *star-struck emoji*

Cece: Shoes! The way to your heart! He does know you!

Sadie: How are things with you and Adelbert? I picked up on some interesting vibes there.

Cece: It's nothing. I hardly see him.

Sadie: Want me to ask Everett to say something to him?

Cece: Please don't. I'm okay. Don't worry about me. You go and keep "consummating" away *laughing emoji* *fire emoji* *clapping hands emoji*

Sadie: Okay. But if you change your mind, tell me.

Cece: Will do. BTW, you two weren't as discreet as you thought you were on that call. You couldn't stop squirming. *laughing emoji* And your blush *winking emoji*

Everett

My hunger for Sadie knows no bounds. The near-constant ache to be inside her, to satisfy her, make her scream my name, is a driving force beating within my chest.

After taking her over my desk, I decide we need to return to a public setting before I listen to my cock again.

While she showers and gets ready, I step out into the bright summer sun to meet Pierce at the door. I compiled a list of items that Sadie might want and arranged for Pierce to collect and drop them here.

"Mr. Ülavere, good to see you again," he greets me impassively, holding the bags I sent for in his large hands.

"Thanks, Pierce. Everything good back at the hotel?" I ask him, not really expecting much of an answer as I scan through the items in the bags.

"All things are running smoothly. I do have one thing to report, though."

At that, my head snaps up. "What's happened?"

Pierce isn't ruffled by much, but his tone suddenly has me on edge, my heart taking on a new rhythm in my chest.

"Your father has been seen walking around the casino. With Alexandra. They have not requested to see you yet. There are a couple of whales staying with us now that we think they might be trying to poach. They have been seen going around to the other casinos and doing the same with high rollers there, offering more amenities and bigger perks."

"Why didn't anyone report on this earlier?" I ask, agitated with myself for not being aware of what's going on in my own casino, postorgasm glow melting away instantly.

"Um"—Pierce shifts uncomfortably and runs a hand across his bald head—"I think mild attempts to contact you have been made today. Perhaps you have been a bit... preoccupied, sir? Sorry, it's not my place to say that." Pierce looks stricken for daring to speak so bluntly.

I'd never fault him for that. His request for formality has always trumped my more lax approach to how we should address each other.

"Don't worry, Pierce. And thank you. I'll be along shortly. Please keep an eye on them and let the staff report if they find anything odd."

"Yes, sir." Accepting my dismissal, he gets in his car and goes back to Auvere to do my bidding.

I really hope my father hasn't caused too much damage to my business by the time I arrive.

I go back in to find Sadie, hoping she'll be pleased with what I've had put together for her.

"What you got there? Went shopping without me?" Sadie asks when she sees me holding the bags.

"I requested some items for you. Didn't think you'd be comfortable walking back into the hotel in only my shirt."

"That's really thoughtful, thanks. I love wearing your shirt, but maybe only around the house. Now, let me see!" she squeals and makes grabby hands for the bags.

Each item she unpacks makes her eyes grow wider and wider. I can hear her heartbeat picking up as her eyes become watery.

"You really get me, don't you?" she asks, shaking her head.

I give her a soft smile. "I'm trying my best. Also, your mood boards are very vivid, and I may have had a look at them over your shoulder when you were scrolling through your phone," I admit, slightly ashamed of myself for violating her privacy, but a little proud at how well I'm getting to know her.

"Well, good thing I don't mind. I don't really have secrets, but that could've caused you a lot of trouble if you were with someone else. Now wait here while I go change, and then you can compliment me on how good I look in the clothes you got me," she says, flipping her hair over her shoulder as she struts off.

I love that she knows how to keep me on my toes, that life is interesting with her. Fun. Sexy. I love that she's confident and that she can be vulnerable with me too, knowing I'll keep her safe.

I love her.

I love Sadie.

The thought is like a slow-rolling wave, softly crashing over me, drenching me in the knowledge of my love for this woman. Falling in love with Sadie was unexpected and all of a sudden.

I don't know when it happened, when our teasing became serious, when our innocent flirting became affection, and when it turned into love.

What I do know is that I love her with all my heart and that I will do anything I can to deserve her love back.

Just as I'm snapping out of my thoughts, contemplating when the right time to tell her is, she steps back into the bedroom.

She looks more beautiful than I could have imagined. "You're exquisite. Do you like it?" I ask as I stare at her, blinking being the only thing my body seems capable of at the moment.

"You mean, do I like the glittery pink mini sheath dress that accentuates my body with its open back and low V front, held together by delicate spaghetti straps? Uh yes, you could say that," she deadpans, her eyes alight with joy. "It looks like the upgraded version of the one I wore when we met. So I'd say you've done pretty well with your selection. Thank you."

She pads over to me and pulls me down by the back of the neck to place a sweet kiss on my lips. It somehow conveys more than just the words she's spoken. I can feel her gratefulness for the dress, for me, just from this kiss.

"Give me a couple of minutes while I tame my hair and fix my face. I'll be ready soon."

Realizing I haven't said much in a while, I stumble out a reply. "I'm going to jump in the shower. There's an issue at the hotel I have to deal with. I'd like to get back there as soon as possible."

"Got it. Basic makeup day. Can do, captain." She gives me a little mock salute, and she's off with one of the bags Pierce brought.

I'm glad my snooping is aiding me so well and that she'll be able to use the cosmetics she likes.

We both finish in record time and leave the safety of the cool house. We step into the late afternoon, blistering summer heat and hurry to get into my car.

"What's happening at the hotel? Anything I can help with?" Sadie asks while looking in the sun visor vanity, applying a raspberry color to her lips.

I can't believe we arrived at my place just yesterday. It feels more like a month. Our relationship has grown to new heights, we've made a commitment to each other, and now we're going to get her belongings to move her in.

"My accidental sperm donor is busy poaching whales at my hotel. I'd love to have a chat with him. He's never been bold enough to come directly into Auvere and approach them in person. It also seems odd that he's there when I'm not," I explain.

"How did he know you won't be there?"

"Remember Alexandra?" She's the only link I can think of, and she's sly enough to pull off such an elaborate plan.

"Do I ever..." she says dryly.

"I'm sure she's paying someone on my staff to report on my movements. They presumably saw us leave yesterday. When we didn't return in the evening, they probably pounced on the opportunity to strike while I'm gone. It's so frustrating." This is the most likely scenario I could come up with.

"What's your father's problem? Can't he just be happy for you for making a success of your life?" Sadie asks the question my younger self asked countless times.

I try to explain the harsh reality of being a dhampir in a community that predominantly consists of vampires. "My entire life, the vampire community has looked down on me for being a dhampir, for being born when I shouldn't have been able to be conceived. I'm a black mark on my father's reputation, my existence a mistake resulting from a night that was supposed to be fun. He makes it a point to remind me that I shouldn't be alive."

"What the fuck is wrong with him? I totally understand why you said I shouldn't meet him. I'd lay into him, give him a piece of my mind for treating you like trash. I'm sorry you have to experience that."

Her vehemence warms my heart, reinforcing my internal admission of love for her. I want to make it a big moment when I tell her I love her, woo her with all the romance I can muster. Driving in a car when I'm this wound up is not quite the right atmosphere I want for such a big declaration. Something I've never said to anyone else in my life.

"You know, in the past, I just ignored him and kind of stayed out of his way. Let him say what he had to say and tried to rise above it. But not tonight. It ends now," I say decisively.

I'm done playing his games.

"What do you need me to do? Distract Alexandra? Bring a knife? Silver bullets? How do vampires fight?" Her serious tone makes me chuckle, and soon we're both falling into fits of laughter.

Sadie makes me feel stronger, bolder, like I can take on any old vampire. Now, I have something—someone—I want to live for. Someone to share my life with. A purpose besides being a thorn in my father's side.

"I just want you to stay safe. Let's grab our stuff from the suite after I'm done and get you moved in at the house. Sound good?"

"Sure. I have a quick errand to run while you're dealing with him. But I'm totally canceling that to get a cheerleader outfit and watch you put that mean fucker in his place. Oh, or boxing gloves! I'm sure I can get them somewhere," she says brightly, holding her fists up in front of her face and shadowboxing.

I laugh at her antics. "I'd love to see you in nothing but boxing gloves, but I'd rather have you as far away from him as possible. I don't want his evil to get anywhere close to your bright."

I know Sadie will support me with whatever I need, but I'd rather have her safe.

Tonight, I'm ready to confront my sire.

Sadie

Everett and I go our separate ways in the lobby, him on a mission to find his evil father, and me to the appointment I scheduled while we were at the house.

Everett has gone so far beyond my expectations that I can't help falling in love with him. He truly understands me, indulges me, and ticks every single one of my boxes. He fucks like a king, but more than that, he makes me feel cherished.

He gave me control in the bedroom when I needed it, and he took control when he needed it. There's something magical about our connection, an understanding between us, a balance that I've never experienced before.

I crave him. His laugh, his teasing, his sweetness, his embrace.

I want to know everything about him, help him accomplish his goals, support him in every endeavor.

I want to make him happy.

I want to give him all the love he deserves.

He's unlocked something in my heart, unlocked a part of me I've been keeping safe my entire life.

I want to prove to him that I'm all in, that he's it for me.

There was a moment last night when I just wanted to tell

him. Wanted to throw it all out in the open, but I held off. I have an idea to show him just how committed I am to him, to building a life together, to loving him.

Pierce meets me in the lobby once Everett is out of sight.

"Good evening, Ms. Sadie. Right this way, please." Pierce leads me to the car.

Once we're both seated, I ask, "Everett won't miss you while we're gone?"

"I think Mr. Ülavere would prefer to handle matters privately tonight. This has been brewing for a long time, and I don't wish to interfere. However, if he requests my presence, I shall have to leave at once and send another car to collect you. I will inform you of all the arrangements, should it be needed," he explains formally.

I wonder if his school was also as focused on speech as Everett's.

"Thanks, Pierce, but I won't be long. They said it'll only take about an hour. And I found the closest place with good reviews that could fit me in. Everett probably thinks I'm shopping, so the timing works out."

The drive is very short, and we find parking right in front of the shop. Feels like luck is on my side today.

"I will wait outside for you. Please call me if you require my assistance with anything," Pierce says as he escorts me to the door.

Everything goes smoothly, and I'm done earlier than expected. I'm giddy with excitement for Everett's reaction when he sees what I did.

The drive back feels longer as I shift uncomfortably in my seat for the entirety of it. Getting out of the car, I say to Pierce, "I'm heading up to the suite to pack. If you bump into Everett first, then let him know. I don't want to message and interrupt his dealings with his father right now."

"Can I escort you up, Ms. Everly?" Pierce asks politely.

I wave him off. "That's okay, thanks, I know where

everything is. Have a good evening, Pierce. And thanks for accompanying me on my top-secret mission."

I feel comfortable and confident as I walk through the lobby. The distance limit between Everett and me may be gone, but a part of him is with me wherever I go, our bond glowing brightly in my chest.

I'm partially distracted trying to decipher Everett's emotions through the bond, so I don't immediately notice the man walking behind me. When I get to the area in front of the private elevator, I can feel his eyes assessing me.

My initial reaction is to think it's just a hotel guest distracted by my glittery ensemble, but my woman's intuition screams predator. That's why when the elevator arrives, I pretend to forget something and start walking back to the lobby.

The man steps in front of me, blocking my way.

"Where's a pretty lady like you running off to?" he purrs creepily.

All the tiny hairs on the back of my neck stand on end, sensing danger, and my heart starts pounding uncomfortably.

Pretending I'm not as affected, I turn in a leisurely fashion and say with a voice full of derision, "Excuse me? Do I know you?"

"Not yet. But I'm hoping that will change. I'd like to get to know you very well."

I shudder at his words, my lip curling up. I hope this man doesn't think his lines will work on anyone. What he thinks sounds smooth just feels oily.

"Yeah, buddy. That's not going to work. I'm taken and very much not interested." I summon all the attitude I've not needed once since I met Everett.

"Oh yeah. I bet I can satisfy you better than he can," the man tries, and I nearly gag at the thought of anyone else touching me but my male.

I give the newcomer a pitying once-over. He's definitely attractive by the world's beauty standards, looks to be in his early forties, dark hair, green eyes... Oh, shit.

"Tell me, loser. How does it feel to want something you can't have?" I ask as things click into place, placing my hands on my hips and letting every inch of my body broadcast the disdain I feel toward him.

"Who says I can't have you?" he dares to ask, trying to look arrogant, but I can see I'm starting to get under his skin.

I smirk back at him and drawl, "I wasn't just talking about me."

His eyes widen in shock the moment understanding hits him.

"I see my son's latest plaything is feisty. I like a challenge."

"You're nothing but a disgusting old vamp. You'll never have me, and you'll never have Everett's hotel. 'Like a challenge,' oh please! You had to come here, behind your son's back, to try to steal his whales. How's that going for you? Business so bad you have to stoop as low as poaching?" I sneer at him.

"Listen here, you little—"

"I'm going to stop you right there." I hold my hand up in front of him, pausing him mid-threat. "I'm sure you have a ton of very creative names to call me. I can assure you, I've heard them all. So save your breath, creepy fucker. What I can tell you is this. Everett is the most amazing person I have ever met. He's smart, generous, kind, thoughtful, and he fucks like a king. You don't deserve to be in his life or even in this hotel. So how about you fuck right off and go back to whatever dark hole you crawled from?"

"Fucks like a king, eh? The boy's young and just a dhampir. I can give you pleasure that only a vampire with my level of experience can provide," he croons, letting his gross gaze slide vulgarly down my body.

"That's what you took from what I said? The fucking part? You're sick. And what makes a vampire any different from a dhampir? How can you be so superior?"

"The way I can let your blood—"

I wave my finger in front of his face. "Nope. Don't even try. Everett sucks my blood perfectly, he makes my whole body sing when he sinks his fangs into me. It's unlike anything I've ever experienced before. And you know what makes it that good?"

His mouth opens to interrupt me, but I cut him off once again before he can spill his filth. My hands accompany all my words, upping their effect as I berate the male.

"No, don't answer, that was rhetorical. Love. I love that male. And I'm pretty sure he loves me. I don't need you. *He* doesn't need you. So this is where we're going to finish our little discussion. I don't want to see you ever again," I finish, chest heaving, my blood nearly boiling with contempt for Everett's father.

"Sadie!"

I turn at hearing Everett's familiar voice. My heart changes its rhythm at recognizing its mate, my sneer transforming to a welcoming smile.

"Hey, zooms. How much did you hear?"

I can tell from his flushed face and balled fists just how angry he is, all of it aimed over my shoulder at the male who played a part in his conception.

"Enough," Everett grits out as he comes to a stop next to me, angling his body slightly in front of mine. To his father, he says, "I told you to get the fuck out of my hotel, and then I find you harassing Sadie? If you don't walk out within the next second, I will pick you up and throw you out myself."

"I was just having a conversation with your little human friend," he says, trying to sound innocent.

"She's my mate," he thunders, each word coming out of him making him appear larger. "You don't get to talk to her. You don't even get to look at her. Get the fuck out!"

The tension in the room is so thick, but I'm also getting really turned on by Everett's protective side. Maybe this is why girls like going to MMA fights.

The next moment, thick, tawny arms band around the old

vampire's chest. He tries to buck against them, but they hold firm. Pierce lifts Everett's father bodily off the floor and carries him out the main door.

I cock my head as I stare after them in amazement, my anger dissipating with every step they take farther from me.

"I didn't even know Pierce was here," I say to Everett, my eyes still trained on the two figures.

"I'm giving him another raise. I totally didn't expect him to step in. He's so mild tempered and incredibly loyal. And incredibly strong," Everett says with a small grin, pride for his friend filling his voice.

Turning to me, he cups my shoulders, stroking his thumbs over my skin. He looks deeply into my eyes as he says, "More importantly, I can't believe how well you put my father in his place just now."

"Sorry if I overstepped, but the audacity of him!"

"I didn't want to interrupt since it looked like you had matters well in hand. You were so sexy," Everett says, biting back his smile.

"Oh yeah? You like how I handled him?" My smile matches his.

"Very much. But I heard you say something specific to him, something that you haven't told me yet." Everett raises his brows in expectation.

"You mean, I did things a bit backward by telling your father that I love you before I told you. Oops. Seems pretty on-brand for us, though." I shrug like it's no big deal I just told him I love him for the first time.

"I think all of our intentions are good, but the order and processes are sometimes mixed up." His face softens. "You know I love you too, right?"

"I thought so. But it's nice to have it confirmed." I beam at him.

"Now, I want to take you somewhere to show you how

much I do love you."

"I'd like that very much. I have a little surprise to show you too."

He threads his fingers through mine and starts walking toward the entrance. "Good surprise or bad surprise?"

"I think you're going to like it. It might just be... Wait, aren't we going upstairs?" I ask in confusion.

I was pretty sure he was about to fuck my brains out while we declare our love for each other.

"Not right now. I want to show you something first," Everett says as he leads me toward his car, which has miraculously appeared in front of the hotel—most likely Pierce's doing.

"You know I've already seen your dick, right?"

"I'm planning to get you very well acquainted again tonight, but this is different. Trust me?" he adds earnestly as he buckles me into my seat.

"Of course. Surprise first, dick later. Got it." To prove I understand, I give him a thumbs-up.

Everett

I'm so unbelievably excited to show Sadie her surprise, not even my father can spoil my mood.

"Any hints about what it is?" Sadie asks, shifting for the umpteenth time in her seat.

At first I thought she was squirming with need, but the scent of her arousal is sitting at a normal level for her. I've gotten so good at gauging her mood that I know the move is not based on a need for friction. *Curious.*

"You get no hints. It'll be too obvious. Just five more minutes," I say as I spot the building down the street from my hotel.

The total drive being less than ten minutes away was one of the major factors for me choosing this place.

"Fine." She pouts, though I can see it's in jest as her lips curve up at the corners.

"Can you tell me about my surprise?" I ask her, imitating her pout.

She giggles at my attempt, the sound so beautiful it makes my cock stir. I reach over to hold her hand for the last minute of the drive, basking in the sweet relief of being done with my father and my past and starting my future with Sadie.

The fates really proved their ingenuity when they made

our paths cross. The ability to also choose our relationship is the cherry on top.

Her brows draw tight as we pull into the empty parking lot of the dark building.

"Sit tight," I tell her, rushing to open her door.

The two-story building's glass facade greets us as we make our way up the stairs. None of the lights are on, but Las Vegas Boulevard is lit up enough that we don't require it.

I pass Sadie the key. "Go ahead, unlock it."

Her brow pulls down even farther, eyes darting around as she searches for a possible explanation for what's happening. I wordlessly encourage her to proceed, pointing with my eyes to the door, and she finally does my bidding.

Walking into the cavernous space, she moves her head from side to side, taking in each detail. From the high ceilings, to the hardwood flooring, to the empty walls. The place is utterly gutted, but I thought it best this way.

"What do you think?" I ask, my heart beating like a bass drum in my chest, my palms clammy.

Her confusion seems to intensify. "What is this place?"

"It's yours."

"To do what with?"

"To open your rental shop. Sparkly stuff for women visiting Vegas."

"You got me a shop?"

"I got you the building. Thought it would be good if you wanted to expand. One side you could have rentals, other side you could have purchases. Maybe add on-site seamstresses for tailoring. I wanted to help you make your dream come true."

Sadie's eyebrows shoot into her hairline, and her jaw drops. She shakes her head as a disbelieving smile takes over her face. "You *bought* me a building? Just like that?"

"Uh... yeah? Is that overstepping?" I grimace, hoping I don't burden her with my slightly extravagant gift.

She walks up to me and cups my cheeks. Tilting my face down to her, she draws me close until our foreheads touch. "This is outrageous. You're outrageous. But you're *my* outrageous male."

Sadie slides her arms around my neck as we pull back just enough to see each other clearly. "You've heard me say it before, but I've got to say it to you again right now. I love you, Everett Ülavere. I've always liked sparkly things, but you're the brightest star in my universe. I can't help but be drawn to you. You eclipse everything and everyone in my life. I'd love you no matter what. Even if the fates hadn't intervened, I believe we would've found each other. I'm excited to stay here with you, to build a life with you, a future."

"Sadie-queen, you stole my words. I had a whole thing planned for how I wanted my love confession to go. I've been working on it all day."

Her chuckle sounds wet as she slides a hand down from around my neck to wipe at a tear tracking down her cheek.

I move one of my hands from her waist to the back of her neck, tilting her face back up to me. "Sadie Eleanor Everly, I love you. Fate might have chosen to push us together, though, if it was up to me, I would choose you for myself. Every time. Every day. I choose you, over and over again—mind, body, soul, heart. It's a fucking privilege to love you, to be loved by you. It feels like I've been living my life in black and white until you arrived with pink and sparkles. I want to make you the happiest woman in the world, help you shine brighter and brighter."

"I hope this goes without saying, but the building isn't the reason I love you. I'd give up all the glittery stuff in my closet, in my future, to be with you."

"Good thing you told me you loved me before I showed you the building. And please keep the glittery stuff."

"In that case, it's time for my surprise."

That makes me perk up, the seriousness of the moment changing with a new kind of energy laden with excitement. I rub my hands together in anticipation.

Sadie looks around the giant room. "Can we move a bit farther back, away from the street?"

"Consider my curiosity piqued, milady. Right this way." I stick my elbow out for her like the day we met and escort her to the back of the room.

There's an alcove behind the counter that's out of view from anyone passing by on the street, and the darkness inside the building provides an extra layer of privacy.

"Would this do?"

"I'd say so. I can still see well enough. Your heightened eyesight will probably be able to make out all the details," Sadie says as she gives me a filthy smirk.

Sadie bends over and sticks her ass out toward me, swatting the hand away that instantly reaches out to touch her. Lifting her dress, she reveals more and more skin until her ass is uncovered. Except for the flimsy string of material covering her pussy, and some film kept in place with tape.

I step closer to look at the film. "What's this?"

"Read it."

"*Bite me*? You got a tattoo that says 'bite me'?"

"It's on the exact spot you bit me the first time. If you don't count the accidental nick. I wanted to show you that I'm all in and good with you drinking my blood. It's actually kind of hot that you only like my blood."

"You got a tattoo for me?" I ask, shock still making my brain and mouth slow.

"Is it too much?" Sadie asks, turning around to face me, eyes widened in concern.

"You know I'm going to marry you, right?" I state more than ask.

Her expression morphs into intrigue. "Is that a proposal?"

"Not yet. That's the one event I'm going to get right. I'm going to romance you so hard that you won't remember that I fucked the order up with all the other wooing."

I already have a ring in mind for her, an argyle pink princess cut I saw while scrolling for earrings I wanted to get her.

Bringing me back to the moment, Sadie says, "I like that we made our own order. It makes our love story special."

"You know what will make it even more special?" I ask, licking my lips as an image comes to mind.

Her expression shifts to something resembling mine. We're clearly very attuned to each other's moods.

"What you got in mind?"

"I think we need to christen your new building."

"I think you're right," Sadie says as she reaches behind her and drags the dress's hidden zipper down. Before it can pool on the floor, she scoops it up and places it neatly on the counter.

Sadie is beautiful standing in front of me in nothing but a tiny triangle covering her cunt and her sexy high heels. I reach forward to rectify the situation and snap the band on either side. I pull it off her, crumpling the fabric up and bringing it to my nose for a deep inhale. My cock is hard and straining for her heat.

"Take my cock out, Sadie-queen," I instruct her through gritted teeth.

She does exactly what I ask, popping the button open and pulling the zipper down before pushing my pants and underwear off. She spits in her hand and smirks at me, daring me to say something.

I let her jerk my cock a couple of times, then lift her up and place her butt on the counter. Making sure she's at the right angle to avoid putting pressure on her fresh tattoo, I scoot her forward just a bit. The counter is at the exact right height for me to line my cock up with her cunt, proving that the fates think of everything.

"This is going to be fast and hard. I'm not going to bite you. I know I can, but I want to show you that I don't just love you because of your blood."

"I never thought it was the only reason, more like an added bonus. I'm totally okay with it."

"Not tonight. I just want your slick cunt to be my sole focus."

"Then what are you waiting for?" Sadie taunts.

I tighten my grip on her thighs as I spread her legs obscenely to watch as she guides me into her wet warmth.

Right there, with Sadie's legs bracketing my hips, her nails clawing at my back, we seal our fate.

Sadie might have tempted me right from the start, but I'm thoroughly enchanted by her now.

Acknowledgements

Thank you for picking up Tempting the Dhampir. I appreciate you for taking a chance on a new author. The world of Alberad and the monsters came to me so easily and I can't wait to share more of the couples with you. Each book is a standalone and will feature a different monster pairing (or pairingS). To each reader who has talked about my book, or interacted with me, thank you for helping me turn this dream into a reality. Each like, comment, and share is like a virtual hug. None of this would be possible without you and I appreciate you more than I can express.

I had a dream team of support behind me, who lifted me up, held my hand, and dried my tears.

Adrienne, thank you for reading those early drafts and each version thereafter. Thank you for loving Sadie and Everett as much as I do, and for letting me prattle on about plot points and helping me iron out the finer details. You're the bestest friend and I couldn't have done this without you.

Colette, thank you for the beautiful cover design, all our sprinting sessions and chats, for helping me with technology, and for talking me through my meltdowns. I appreciate you.

My beta team: TB Wiese, Hazel Mack, Elisha Kemp, and Bella Blair. Thank you for lending your heaps of experience and for all your input with this book. I appreciate the time you took out of writing your own stories to help me with mine.

Allie, thank you for the numerous voice notes to explain the Kentucky schooling system to me and what life as a teacher is like.

Your students are lucky to have you.

Mon Reyes, thank you for the beautiful cover and being the first reason readers will pick up the book. You captured Everett and Sadie so well and I can't wait to continue the rest of the series with you.

Jeanine, thank you for smoothing out my writing and getting rid of all those dangling modifiers. I've learned so much from you and appreciate how thorough you are.

To my husband who is my biggest champion. Thank you for your continuous encouragement and never doubting me. You are my pillar of strength and the master of Korean admin. I love you.

And finally and most importantly, to each reader who has talked about my book, or interacted with me, thank you for helping me turn this dream into a reality. Each like, comment, and share is like a virtual hug. None of this would be possible without you and I appreciate you more than I can express.

—Elle

P.S. I'd love to hear from you, so please don't hesitate to contact me.

If you haven't done so already, please consider leaving a rating and review for my debut novel. They're the lifeline of indie authors and will help me get a foothold in the wonderful world of smutty and funny ebooks.

About the Author

Elle Sterling is a monster and paranormal author based in South Korea.

Her stories are fun and flirty, filled with heart and spice. HEAs guaranteed.

Much like her own life after emigrating from South Africa, she enjoys writing characters crossing cultural barriers and loving without restraint.

You can usually find Elle in her writing cave with coffee within reach at all times. She also enjoys grilled kimchi-and-cheese sandwiches and hibernates during the humid summer until the weather has cooled.

Elle loves connecting with readers, so visit her on social media or email elle@ellesterling.com

Elle Sterling

www.ingramcontent.com/pod-product-compliance
Lightning Source LLC
Chambersburg PA
CBHW031254160726
47993CB00001B/155